Mary Alice Peale

Philadelphia, 1777

—∞∞∞—

by Kathleen Duey

Andrea Landis
(215) 997-9075

—∞∞∞—

Aladdin Paperbacks

For Richard
For Ever

First Aladdin Paperbacks edition August 1996
Copyright © 1996 by Kathleen Duey

Aladdin Paperbacks
An imprint of Simon & Schuster
Children's Publishing Division
1230 Avenue of the Americas
New York, NY 10020

The text of this book is set in Fairfield Medium.
Printed and bound in the United States of America
10 9 8

Library of Congress Cataloging-in-Publication Data
Duey, Kathleen
Mary Alice Peale, Philadelphia, 1777 / by Kathleen Duey.
p.   cm. — (American diaries; #4)
Summary: When her wounded brother returns from battle,
twelve-year-old Mary must get help for him without telling her
father, a wealthy Tory, who has disowned his son for joining
General Washington's Continental Army.
ISBN 0-689-80387-7
1. United States—History—Revolution, 1775–1783—Juvenile
fiction.   [1. United States—History—Revolution, 1775–1783—
Fiction.]   I. Title. II. Series.
PZ7.D8694Mar   1996
[Fic]—dc20
96-16052

October 6, 1777
Philadelphia

General Howe's British officers swagger about everywhere. Yesterday, in the carriage with Mother, I saw two of them shouting at a miller with a wagon load of flour from Chestnut Hill—his wheels had splashed mud on their fine red coats.

All the men are in an uproar, arguing about the Germantown battle north of the city two days ago. Father says Washington's army was forced to a ragged retreat. But tavern talk spills out into the street, and there are loud debates. We could hear musket fire again this morning and no one knew what it meant. The war frightens me. I cannot stop thinking about William.

The city is quieter now that the British are here, at least. Before Howe's army came in September, the gutters were filled with patriot broadsides and pamphlets; the rebels stood on corners, shouting out speeches where anyone would listen. I was afraid the mobs of last July would rise again and this time do more than throw stones through our windows. Now, the patriots are mostly gone, having left in darkness when Howe's men marched in.

Father is entirely loyal to King George III. He says that William will never be welcome home again now that he is a soldier for the rebellion. Father is cordial to Howe's officers, even though he knows William could be killed by any one of them today, tomorrow, or a month from now. It seems wrong to me that we must obey a king who lives half the world away, and even more wrong to host his soldiers. Would Father disown me if he knew my thoughts?

As I write about the war, with all the many dead and hurt, Mother has the servants running, busily readying the house for her ball tonight. Tories and Loyalists all over the city have entertained the British officers and she is not to be outdone. So, while my own dearest brother and the other Continentals are perhaps bleeding and dying, my mother discusses brocade and silk with her dressmaker, and my elder sister Abigale flirts with her British colonel. The world has turned upside down.

CHAPTER ONE

"Mary Alice Peale!"

Startled by her sister's voice, Mary finished shaking pounce onto the wet ink. She set down her little silver sander. Abigale was just outside her door, sounding as impatient and demanding as she had all week long. Mary snuffed her candle, removing the gray tail of burned wick that would start to smoke soon. The flame bounced back up, brighter. Then she blew the gritty pounce from her open diary page. The ink was dry.

"Mary?"

Mary closed her diary and slid out of her

writing desk. She quickly tucked the diary into her clothespress, on a low shelf behind her fresh chemises and stockings. Standing, she noticed a dusting of pounce on the edge of Florence's bed. She brushed it off, blew out her candle, and turned toward the door.

"Mary!"

Abigale sounded furious. Mary smoothed her skirt and straightened her lace cap. Only then did she open the door and step out into the hall. Abigale was standing with her hands on her hips. "Mrs. Francis is waiting for you."

Mary looked toward the last room at the end of the hall. It had been a bedchamber before her three older sisters had married and moved out. Now it was the fitting and sewing room—or the wreath-making room or the place where her mother and the servants laid out fat green pears to ripen. For a few weeks, it had been a billeting room for three of General Howe's British soldiers, but they had found quarters more to their taste, closer to Front Street where the taverns were.

"Come along, Mary," Abigale insisted.

Mary shook her head. "You take your turn first. I will do it later. I—"

Abigale cut her off with an impatient gesture. "No, Mary, *now*."

Abigale was wearing only her chemise and stays, covered with a thin robe. She was sixteen, four years older than Mary, with dark hair and white skin Mary envied. Her own gingery hair and freckles were not likely to turn any heads when she was older.

Framed by the doorway of Abigale's bed-chamber, Mary could see, laid out across the bed, the deep green brocade dress her beautiful sister would wear that evening. The long, pointed bodice was laced over the pearl white underskirt and petti-coat; the panniers on the skirt flared out and would accent Abigale's hips, the green river of silk draping in crescents to the floor. It was perfect. Abigale would charm her British colonel.

"Mary!" Abigale kept her voice low, but she was talking between clenched teeth. "Mrs. Francis wants you first. She has some reason . . . and she insists. Now come along."

"The sun is barely risen. I want a cup of cider and—"

"*After* you finish," Abigale cut her off. "I will not let you spoil this evening for me."

Mary pressed her lips together. She had been relieved when the British soldiers had decided to billet somewhere else, and she didn't want British officers dancing in their ballroom. She didn't want to watch Abigale and her friends giggling coyly whenever one of the younger officers said something clever.

"No one would miss me if I simply stayed in my room this evening, Abigale." She had already stood patiently while Mrs. Francis had cut down her mother's yellow silk watteau, making sure the bodice fit, that the flounces fell perfectly, exposing the patterned quilting of the petticoat. Now it would be another half hour of standing while the hems were pinned. And all this so she could spend an evening laced up in stays so tight she couldn't breathe, to impress the men who were trying to kill her brother? William was barely eighteen. The thought of him dying made Mary shiver.

Abigale scowled at her, then instantly relaxed her face, remembering that extreme expressions were bad for her complexion. "You will *not* ruin this evening for me," she said slowly and evenly. "Peggy Chew is coming, and some of her friends. We are all upset about William, but—"

"Mistress Abigale?"

The voice came from behind Mary and she turned to see David Spague, his thin face tense and unhappy. Florence and the kitchen girls must have been busy or her mother would never have asked him to carry a message in the household—he had his own work, out in the carriage house. "Madam Peale requests that you join her in the ballroom," David recited in a flat, uncomfortable voice.

Mary heard Abigale exhale, a little explosion of impatience. "Can't Mother manage without me?"

"Both of you." David kept his eyes fastened on the pine plank floor as he spoke. "Both of you are to come."

Mary glanced at her sister; Abigale could be so rude. Mary liked David. He had been indentured to her father at the age of seven. Now, at ten, he still had a hungry, too-thin look, like a Front Street orphan, even after three years of Rachel's good cooking. He fingered the buckle on his maroon breeches, obviously nervous, but Abigale let him squirm.

"Tell Mother she can simply manage alone for another hour or two," she said at last.

"Don't make him do that," Mary objected. "Mother will be cross with him, then."

David shifted, but did not take his eyes from the smooth pine floor planks. He lived out in the carriage house now. Samuel was teaching him to drive the carriages and care for the harness and horses. Mary knew that being pressed into house service like this was a blow to his pride. If it hadn't been improper for her to chide her selfish sister in front of a servant, she would have. Davey was always kind to everyone and everything. He cared for the stable cats and the chickens and their cow. He had nursed a tiny bird once, and it had gotten well.

Abigale shook her head. Her waterfall of curls brushed her shoulders. "David is bound in Father's service, Mary, and he will do as I say. Give your mistress my reply," she instructed David, then focused her attention on Mary again. "You have one minute to get in here. If Mrs. Francis gets upset, I will hold you responsible." Abigale whirled around and disappeared into the fitting room, closing the door behind herself.

"Why are you being sent with messages in the house today, Davey?" Mary asked once Abigale was gone. For the first time David looked up and met her eyes.

"I was in the kitchen asking Rachel for an apple for the new gelding and your mother passed me. Your father and some others are arguing again," he added softly. "In the front parlor."

"Who?" Mary kept her voice as low as he had.

"Master Gilliam, the Quaker, and that old British gentleman. The tanner."

Mary nodded. "I know who you mean. Robert Wite. The one who thinks the whole of the

Continental Army should be hauled back to England, every one, to be hanged."

"That one. His breath stinks."

Mary couldn't suppress a smile. "Did you hear anything?"

David nodded. "They said that Washington's Continentals ran like rabbits at Germantown. But they are all old men, and Tories. In the street it is told differently."

Mary waited as David looked up and down the long hall. Then he stepped closer and whispered. "They say the redcoats were on the run, but Washington's generals got confused in the fog and dark, and that one attacked another's rear guard. That's what ruined the advance. If not for that, the Continental Army might have won."

Mary drew in a breath, imagining. If Washington's Continentals had won, the British would have been driven out of Philadelphia. She almost said it aloud, then saw the disquiet on David's face. Whatever her father's punishments for such seditious talk, it would go far worse for Davey than it would for her. "Rachel says many of the shops down by the Shambles were closed up and dark last Wednesday when she went for vegetables and meat."

Davey nodded. Then his face brightened.

"Have you seen the new gelding?" His voice went soft, reverent. "He's a beauty, all gloss and spirit. He let me feed him an apple last evening."

Mary nodded, smiling at him. Her father had found the perfect work for David; he loved the horses as much as Samuel did. "Father mentioned the horse at last dinner. He was quite proud of him."

David's eyes sparkled. "The gelding won't let Samuel near him. Nor anyone else. He's fiery."

Mary glanced toward the fitting room door. "I must go in, Davey. What is it my mother cannot do without immediate help?"

Davey squared his shoulders. "I think she just wants someone to approve of the decorations. They have hung a flower and ribbon festoon along the railing and the floor gleams like glass."

"I could go admire the ballroom," Mary said slowly, considering. David seemed to understand that she was thinking aloud; he did not respond but merely waited. Mary shook her head. "But Abigale will make a row about the fitting. Mrs. Francis is so easily upset lately."

David lifted his chin. "What shall I tell her, then?" His eyes crossed Mary's face, then went back to the floor in a movement so swift and fluid that anyone who was not watching him carefully would not have noticed. Mary knew all he wanted was to be out the kitchen door and across the gardens, back to the carriage house and the stables.

Mary smiled at him. "Say you found us in the fitting room wrapped in silk and stuck full of pins. Say I will come in half an hour."

David flashed her one of his rare smiles, then turned about and very nearly ran back up the hall. Mary saw him slip a little on the polished wood as he turned the corner, heading toward the wide stairway that led down to the ground floor of the house.

The fitting room door clicked open. "What are you *doing*?" Abigale demanded. Mary spun around, startled. Abigale had opened the door wide enough to peek out.

"I was just coming."

Abigale let out another little burst of impatient breath, then whispered. "Mary, Mrs. Francis is *waiting*. She is the only seamstress in Philadelphia who can properly sew a pinked and plaited *falbala*, and her ruched roses are beyond compare. And," Abigale added, barely whispering the words, "rumor says she is Peggy Chew's tailoress. It won't do to offend her."

Mary nodded, staring into her sister's face. Abigale rarely managed a conversation without tossing in two or three words of French and an exaggerated inflection. Mary thought it sounded silly, but Abigale's admirers apparently found it attractive. Her British colonel looked thunderstruck whenever he was close to her.

Abigale led Mary into the fitting room. "Here she is, Mrs. Francis. She did not mean to keep you waiting, I am sure."

"I do apologize," Mary said, dropping a curtsy to please Abigale. Instead she earned a quick frown. Mary sighed. Perhaps at twelve she was too old to curtsy to a tailoress.

Mrs. Francis was standing beside the hemming platform with a pincushion in one hand and an impatient, questioning expression on her face. She was a heavyset woman, and her dress, as it always did, reflected the latest styles from France. People said she knew dressmakers in Paris who sent her miniatures of new and interesting fashions before the seamstresses in Boston or New York had any idea what was to come.

"I have three other houses to visit today, Mistress Mary," Mrs. Francis said tightly. "There are a number of balls being planned."

Mary saw Abigale gesturing urgently and forced herself to smile. "I apologize sincerely for my delay," she said in her most polite voice. She stepped up onto the platform and smiled again, but it was only to please Abigale. Mary hated this. The last four times, Mrs. Francis had pricked her lightly with a pin if she moved around too much. Mary was quite certain she did it on purpose.

"Is your husband well?" Abigale asked pleasantly after a moment or two had passed.

Mrs. Francis looked around sharply. "What?"

Abigale blushed. "I don't mean to intrude. It was just that . . . I recalled that last time you said he was suffering with a winter cough and had not been able to leave the house."

Mrs. Francis smiled quickly. "So I did, so I did. He is somewhat better, but still in bed. The doctor bled him last week again. Ten ounces." She was frowning as she straightened out her pins and chalks and set to work.

Mary tried to hold still, wondering if Mrs. Francis's husband was really sick. If he was, she would be worried, of course. But perhaps he was off with Washington's Continental Army and the tale of his sickness was to explain his absence. Families all over the city were trying to hide any tie they had with Washington's rebels. Mary had heard her own mother telling a guest that William was away hunting with friends rather than admit he had gone to join Washington's army.

Mary was careful not to move as Mrs. Francis

pinned her petticoat hemline and then slid the yellow silk watteau over her head. The seamstress pulled the loose drapes of the cloth until it fell correctly, the front a cascading, open V that showed off the quilted petticoat beneath.

Abigale was humming to herself as she fingered the embroidered edge of her petticoat, laid out over the table in the middle of the room. She began to sway as though she were dancing.

Mary shifted and Mrs. Francis looked up, frowning.

"I'm sorry," Mary said quickly. Mrs. Francis didn't answer as she bent back to her work, but Mary saw her glance at Abigale and something dark crossed her face. Was Mrs. Francis upset by the war? By the way the city had opened its arms to the British? Abigale went on with her humming, her dreamy swaying. Mary watched her. More than anything Mary wanted to see William, to know that he was safe. For an awful instant she imagined him lying wounded, his usually merry face still and white. Her eyes flooded with tears. William had talked to her about the war before he had left. He never acted like she was too young or too foolish to understand things. Abigale did not notice when Mary wiped her eyes. Mrs. Francis did not pause in her pinning.

While Mary put her everyday gown back on, Abigale was looking at the sample cards. Each one held a few inches of decorative work: ruched roses, a miniature plaited flounce, pinked edging set in a tiny curved wave. Mary felt a rush of irritation. There was no time for Abigale to change her mind about any of the adornments on the green gown she would wear tonight. She was already thinking about the next ball.

"I want you to be charming this evening," Abigale said suddenly, looking up. "I can't tell you how important this is to me. I want so badly to impress them."

"Them?" Mary asked, confused.

Abigale flushed prettily. "The English officers."

"I thought you liked Colonel—" Mary broke off, unable to recall the man's name.

"Farringcote," Abigale finished for her. "I do. But no more than several of the others. Mary, please," Abigale went on breathlessly. "Just don't be a sour-face tonight. I know you are worried about William. So am I. But it doesn't have to spoil this evening."

Mary looked into her sister's face, trying to understand. How could worry over William *not* spoil an evening of dancing with the men who were trying to kill him?

CHAPTER TWO

Once she was out in the hall, Mary ran lightly in her stocking feet toward the ballroom, carrying her shoes. She slid to a stop at the main staircase landing, listening, trying to hear the voices of the men in the front parlor below. She sat on the top step to put on her shoes. She had barely gotten the second one buckled when she heard her father's voice.

"Mary?"

Mary stood up. Her parents' bedchamber was across the hall from the fitting room, but her father almost never came upstairs in the daytime. Had he heard her running down the hall?

"Yes, Father?" She turned.

He was fingering his lace jabot, a look of amusement in his light blue eyes. "And where are you going in such haste?"

Mary blushed. "Mother wanted me in the ballroom."

"Then you should certainly attend her." He smiled.

Mary longed to ask him about the war, about what his friends had said. "Davey said there were guests this morning," she began cautiously.

Her father nodded. "We spent much time in talking. Robert Wite criticized the balls everyone is giving. He says we should all be careful of our money, that the king is going to need every shilling of it to win this war. John Gilliam, of course, opposes the war entirely."

Mary thought about John Gilliam. He was a sober-faced man, someone her father greatly admired for his industry and the sensible management of his sawmills up in Chestnut Hill. He was a strict Quaker, very much against the war. He did not believe in killing for any reason. He opposed anyone taking up arms against the British, the Indians, the Hessian mercenary soldiers hired by the king—or anyone else for that matter.

"Mr. Gilliam says there are more Free Quakers

than you would think, though," Mary's father went on, watching her face closely. "He says quite a number of them have joined Washington now, even though their fellows keep them out of Sunday meeting for it. Washington's army is growing." Her father smiled. "Is that enough news for you, Miss Nosy?"

Mary decided to risk a question. "Are the Continentals winning then, sir?"

Her father laughed and touched his hair. He had stopped wearing a wig except for formal occasions about a year before, but he still kept his own hair carefully powdered. Little flecks of white talc clung to his fingers. He shook his head. "No. Nor is there any chance that they will. They put up more of a fight at Germantown than anyone thought, but they stepped on their own coattails in the end. That drunken idiot General Stephens attacked his own compatriots in the fog. They retreated like the scoundrels they are." He shook his head and a darkness passed through his eyes.

Mary's heart constricted and she could not stop the question from rushing out. "Do you suppose William was—"

"I do not wish to hear that name, Mary," her father interrupted her. "He is a fool. Worse than a fool. And he is no longer a son of mine."

"But Father—"

"No man of honor betrays his king," Mary's father said tersely. "And there's an end on it. I will hear no more." He looked past her, out the window above the staircase. "A fine day today." He lowered his eyes to meet hers again. "It won't be long before all this strife and confusion are behind us. King George has no choice but to settle it quickly. Matters in Europe demand his attention as well."

He was silent for so long that Mary wondered if he had forgotten she was there. His face was set, his eyes remote.

"I suppose Mother will be waiting," she said timidly.

"Go, then, but with a bit more seemly manner. Are you finishing your sampler?"

Mary exhaled slowly. He wasn't angry. He was smiling at her. "Yes. I work on it almost every day, Father. Some of the stitches are difficult."

"Fine embroidery is a charming accomplishment in a wife, Mary," he said, still smiling. "Do your best to learn it."

"Yes, Father." Mary gathered up her petticoats and tried to make a ladylike crossing of the stairway landing, following the hall around the corner past the workroom, grateful that she was so soon out of her father's sight. She kept one hand on her petticoats even once she knew he couldn't see her, trying to carry herself the way her mother did, with a calm, stately grace.

Mary arrived in the ballroom, still walking like a lady. Her mother smiled. "Mary, at last. I had begun to think you and Abigale had both changed your minds about your gowns, and poor Mrs. Francis would be here until evening." She looked past Mary, arching her brows, one hand daintily holding her painted silk fan. "Where is Abigale?"

Mary shook her head. "I left before she was finished. I didn't want you to have to wait any longer."

"How considerate of you." Mary's mother leaned forward to straighten the lace cap pinned into Mary's reddish curls. "You left a little too quickly," she admonished gently. "Your cap is as crooked as a kitchen girl's."

"What did you want to show us?" Mary asked, stepping back from her mother's perfumed touch.

"All of this!" her mother said in a light, breathy voice. She swept her hand up in a gesture that encompassed the railing entwined with silk flowers and vines, the shining floor, the swags of beribboned greenery that hung in curves between one tall window and the next. "Isn't it lovely?"

"It is, Mother," Mary said in the most enthusiastic voice she could manage. If her mother noticed the strain in her manner, she said nothing.

A shout rang out in front of the house. Mary went to peer from the window. Below, a cart piled high with logs had stopped at the end of the stone walk. The driver sat, looking up toward the porch. Mary heard a great banging on the front door. "It's the wood corders, Mother."

"Florence will send David to show them where to stack it," Mary's mother said from behind her. "I wanted to make sure we had enough. Tonight I want to use only wood, so the scent of the pine boughs in the swags isn't ruined by the odor of coal smoke."

Mary nodded. It was the kind of special touch her mother was known for. Her entertainments were always well regarded and often imitated. Mary watched the wood corder come back down the stone walk. Her mother had been right. David Spague was tagging along just behind him. David stopped beside the cart and spoke to the driver, patting the team of horses. He gestured, indicating that the wagon should go around to the back of the house. That would mean going to the corner, then up Spruce Street to Fifth. Even though Peale House was a separate building—not like the row town houses that were so common closer to the river in Society Hill—there was no way to drive a wagon from the front of the house to the back. The wagoner would have to go all the way around the block to the little dirt drive that led past the carriage house into the backyard.

The driver whipped up his horse, starting the wagon rolling. Mary could hear the grind of the iron wheel rims against the smooth Belgian block that paved the street.

Mary turned. Her mother had a little frown of concern on her face. "Do you think the swags are too much?"

Mary shook her head quickly. She could not say what she thought. The whole thing was too much; it was wrong to have a ball while there were battles a few miles from their door, while William was in danger. A knock on the frame of the open door made them both turn. It was their housekeeper, Florence Maccaby. "The logs have arrived, madam?" she said. Florence still had a touch of her Scots accent. She had a habit of making statements sound like questions, her voice rising at the end of every sentence.

Mary's mother nodded curtly. "Tell them to carry the hearth log in. Rachel is ready for it. And we want logs in both parlors. Lay a fire in here, too, but we won't light it until later."

Florence turned to leave. "Yes, mistress."

Mary listened to her heavy step as she went down the hallway. The step hesitated, then stopped. Mary heard her father's voice. "Florence? Is that the fire logs? Have them stack what isn't needed tonight along the garden shed wall. Send David out. He can show them."

"I have already done that, sir." Florence's ponderous footfalls went on down the stairs. A moment later, Mary's father appeared in the doorway.

"It is attractive, isn't it?" Mary's mother asked, her voice bright, cheerful.

Mary's father looked absently at the decorations. "It's very pretty, my dear." He looked around once more without comment, then faced Mary's mother again. "I have work in my account books to complete," he added after a moment. "I have to manage the loss from the last pirated cargo. Benjamin and I will be at it for hours." Mary saw a look of pain cross her mother's face as he left.

"I am so very weary of this war. No one can trade, or travel, or live without danger. And I worry so for William," she said, almost under her breath. "But your father will not even consider trying to find him. . . ." She trailed off and did not finish, turning her head, but not quickly enough. Mary saw her eyes fill with tears.

Mary didn't know what to say. The sounds of

the men unloading the firewood filtered in through the open windows on the far end of the ballroom overlooking the backyard. One of them cursed. If Mary's mother heard, she gave no sign.

"I would just like this evening to be lovely," she said. "To be like it ought to be. It's Abigale's first real ball in Peale House." She slapped her fan against her palm. "But instead we have this war. Oh, how I hate it."

CHAPTER THREE

"Mistress?" It was David Spague, standing in the arched doorway.

Mary's mother turned, startled. "Yes, David?"

"They want to know, should they bring in the wood through the rear quarters?"

"Of course," Mary's mother said, keeping her face slightly turned to hide her emotions from David. "And tell Samuel I will want the carriage this afternoon. I will let him know." Her voice sounded brusque and Mary knew that David would assume he had done something to displease her. She would have to tell him later that her mother had been upset before he arrived. Mary looked longingly at the golden autumn sunshine outside the windows.

"You could watch them unload the wood from the storeroom window in the back quarters, if you like," her mother said, her voice flat. Mary knew she was being chided, that her mother would rather she stayed.

"I would like to," Mary began cautiously.

Her mother dismissed her with an impatient wave of her hand. "Go, then, Mary." She gestured to the rosewood pianoforte in the corner of the room. "Abigale will play a piece this evening and will be down soon to practice. She will want an audience. We shall have a pianist and a harpist tonight, as well as two violins."

Mary nodded and shifted her weight from one foot to the other. "Go," her mother shooed, but she was smiling now. "You haven't heard a word I've said."

Mary left the ballroom like a lady, her head high, her spine straight, her hand resting lightly on the fullest part of her skirt, ready to gather the stiff petticoats if need be. Across the landing, she glanced back toward the ballroom. Her mother could not see her. She relaxed her posture as much as her stays allowed and hurried down the staircase.

At the bottom of the long stairs, she turned

toward the back of the house, crossing the entry with its arches and plastered ceilings decorated with vines, shells, and circles of leaves. She followed the ground-floor hall past the front and back parlors, then past the little room where the family sometimes ate.

Mary heard someone humming quietly and looked through the open door to see Rachel bent over one of the drop-leaf tables, rubbing at the wood with an oiled rag.

"Isn't that Florence's work?" Mary asked. Rachel looked at her, her eyes guarded. Mary hastened to put her at ease.

"I only wondered. It makes no difference to me who does it, or to Mother, I should think."

Rachel smiled a little. "Usually Florence does this, Mistress Mary. I just asked her to turn the spit of venison for me while I got out of the heat for a few minutes."

In winter, the warming kitchen was comfortable—the nicest, warmest room in the house. Mary would often take her sampler there and sit on the wall bench, practicing her stitches while Rachel cooked. But the rest of the year the heat of the enormous hearth was unwelcome. Then the warming kitchen became an inferno and Rachel's face would stream with sweat.

"I used coal today for all the early baking."

Mary nodded. Coal burned a lot hotter than wood. She looked at Rachel more closely. Her smooth coffee-colored skin was flushed rose brown from hovering close to the clay beehive bake oven that took up one corner of the hearth.

"My little Francine said to tell you hello," Rachel said, smiling. Her teeth always looked impossibly white to Mary, perfect and pretty. Many of the adults she knew had weak, brownish teeth. Rachel smiled wider. "Francy wants to know when you can give her another reading lesson."

"Return her greeting, please," Mary said. "We can have a lesson whenever she likes." Mary trailed off, caught in a rush of emotion. William had taught her to read. He had been infinitely patient, repeating the letters a hundred times. And he had promised to show her how to do arithmetic. Now, perhaps, no one ever would. Mary realized Rachel was still waiting for her to respond. "Bring her with you one day and we can read," Mary finished lamely, hoping Rachel wouldn't notice how upset she was. "I was just thinking . . ." she added, then couldn't finish.

Rachel smiled, her eyes soft and kind. "You are thinking about William," she said kindly. "Your poor mother is just pinched in the middle of this. And so are you."

"I'm going to watch them unload the wood from the storeroom," Mary said quickly, to end the conversation. Her mother would be angry if she knew she was talking about family affairs with the servants. Even Rachel.

"You had better hurry then," Rachel said, smiling broadly. If she had noticed Mary's sudden coolness, she had understood it—or was ignoring it. Either way, Mary was grateful. She opened the heavy storeroom door. This was one of her favorite places in the whole house. It was quiet, and it smelled of the baskets of apples along one wall. There were potatoes, too, and a side of dark venison hanging from a chain. Six or seven plucked chickens dangled next to it. Sacks of flour stood near the door. The upper frame of the window was propped open. This room was kept chilly on purpose. Mary leaned her forehead against the cool glass.

Below, in the rear yard, the men were angling the cart, backing the horses slowly over the grass. The tall wood corder was walking alongside the wagon, calling out instructions to the driver.

David was standing close to the garden shed, watching the creaking progress of the wagon. He looked up briefly and saw Mary. He waved and she waved back at him, envying him for a second. He was indentured and had to do what his master and mistress instructed him to do. But he was free to go outside, and he got to do errands all over the city for Samuel and her father. And when his indenture was up, he would be free to leave the Peales' house and do what he wanted to in the world.

The driver had backed the cart through the shrubs and trees and flowers so that the wood-spoked wheels rested just at the foot of the back-door steps. The horses stood blowing clouds of steamy breath into the air as the driver climbed down, grinning at his partner. Not a single rosebush or vegetable bed had been hurt in the least.

David stepped forward and talked to the men, pointing at the door to the back quarters. The men nodded and set to work. David joined them, probably hoping that one of them would give him a penny or two. David was saving all he could for his day of freedom.

The men unloaded the kitchen log first. It took both of them to carry it into the house, with David holding the door wide and shouting a warning to Rachel and Florence. Walking slowly, the men came into the kitchen. Mary turned from the window to follow them, watching as they let the log settle heavily onto the andirons in the massive hearth. Rachel had moved the heavy iron pots aside, setting the spit and the crane high enough so the enormous log could fit beneath it. The men lowered it onto the fire, leaning in, scarcely ducking their heads, their thick leather boots getting a dusting of ash from the edges of the fire.

Then they brought in smaller pieces of wood and filled the wood boxes along the wall. As the men began carrying the fragrant pine logs to the other rooms, Mary went back to the window, watching them go in and out until they were finished. The wagon creaked and swayed, leaving the yard.

"Emily? Bring your wash bucket and rags in here, quickly!" Mary's mother called down the hall. Mary heard a faint reply and peeked into the hall. Her mother was staring in distaste at the pieces of bark and muddy boot prints left by the wood corders. While her mother was turned, looking toward the back parlor where Emily's voice had come from, Mary ducked into the room across the hall.

Mary stood still for a second, breathing as quietly as she could. She hadn't been in this room since William had left. She listened. There was no sound from the hallway except Emily's cheerful, bantering voice teasing Rachel about something. Rachel laughed and then they were both quiet. Mary was pretty sure her mother was gone. The servants rarely joked in her presence.

Mary looked around. She loved this little room. It had once been part of the back quarters. When her three older sisters had still been at home, they had had a children's nurse. This had been her bedchamber. Then, as the girls got married and William got older, it had been his bedchamber. Mary's father had had the bed removed in his initial fury after William left. Now the room looked like a plain, small parlor. The wallpaper was a clear, vibrant blue. The wainscoting had been painted a darker blue, and there was a beautiful pier glass between the windows. One window was raised slightly, probably to give the room an airing.

Mary felt tears pressing against her eyelids. Her father had called in the plasterers and painters within a week of William's departure. He could have waited. He could have left this room alone.

Mary looked at the hearth. Someone had laid a fire. Maybe her mother had decided to use this room for conversation away from the dancers and the music. The idea of British officers in William's bedchamber made Mary feel sick.

"Mary?" Her mother came in, fan still in her right hand, her left hand fluttering delicately over her own throat. "I thought I saw you come in here. Whatever are you doing?"

"Nothing," Mary said quickly.

Her mother came to stand beside her. "I'm going down past the Shambles to get your father's wig for this evening. He left it at the peruke maker's for cleaning and repair and now has no time to get it himself. We will stop also at the chandler's on Union Street. I want more molded bayberry candles for tonight." She looked around the room. "You need fresh air, too, I think."

Mary nodded, eager to go, to get away from Peale House for an hour or two. "Will Abigale come?"

Mary's mother shook her head. "The hairdresser will be here soon. You are sure you don't want yours arranged?"

"Florence does it well enough." Mary didn't like the idea of someone turning her hair into a ratted and switched mound of curls that made her look like a stranger to herself in the looking glass. Abigale always looked so *different*.

Mary's mother sighed. "Abigale will spend the whole day preparing. A nap. Cold water on her face and throat to make her skin glow. Florence finished pressing the gowns yesterday and she is doing the underskirts and petticoats now. I assume the yellow silk fit well after Mrs. Francis cut it down?"

Mary nodded, then glanced back out the window in time to see David walking like a thief, easing his way around the side of the garden shed, his eyes moving constantly. She watched, puzzled.

"I thought about having a fire in here this evening," Mary's mother said. Then she shook her head. "I am afraid that if we give the men a room, they will spend the whole evening refighting the battle of Germantown instead of dancing."

Mary hadn't thought of that. Perhaps she could overhear news of the war tonight while the British officers tried to dance and bow their way into Abigale's affections. For the first time she felt a little stir of interest in the ball.

"I do so want this to be nice for Abigale," Mary's mother said. "Your sisters had lovely parties when they were Abigale's age. I hope she can find a husband among these young men."

Mary nodded. Her eldest sister, Becky, was twenty-six now, Victoria was twenty-four, and Lizzie was about to turn twenty-three. They had all made good marriages and seemed happy enough. When they came to visit they talked endlessly about their households, their husbands, their pregnancies. Victoria had just had a baby, her second girl, about two weeks before. She would not be coming to the ball this evening. Nor would Becky, of course. She and her husband could not travel all the way from New York for a ball. Lizzie's headaches seemed to worsen in the autumn and winter—but if she felt well enough, she might come. Mary felt a stab of loneliness. "I miss them."

"I miss your sisters, too. And Becky most of all," Mary's mother said, as though she had felt it as well. Mary nodded, hearing the worry in her mother's voice. Becky was usually a sunny person, cheerful and good-hearted. But her last letter had been glum. She didn't like living in New York. It was so much smaller than Philadelphia, and not nearly as cultured.

"I want you to have a wonderful social season when your time comes." Mary's mother touched her hair with a gentle hand. "Perhaps we can all be together again soon." Mary knew she was thinking about William—but neither of them said anything. "Run up and get your shawl. I will be in the kitchen."

Mary nodded, but after her mother left, she stood still, wishing that everything could be the way it had been when she was little. She wanted William to come bursting through the door and swoop her up and spin her around until she was dizzy. She wanted her sisters to come home. She wanted the war to end.

Mary stared out the window. Davey was coming out of the garden shed. Without looking back at the house, he started across the gardens to the stables. He was very nearly running. Mary shook her head. Davey had most likely hidden something in the shed that he didn't want anyone to find. Knowing Davey, it would be a bird's nest, or perhaps some stray kitten.

Mary sighed. When she got home, she would find a way to sneak out to the garden shed to see what Davey was hiding there. If it was a kitten or some such pet, she would talk her mother into letting him keep it. Mary smiled a little, feeling a pleasant sense of anticipation. Maybe Davey had found a puppy or a baby rabbit.

Mary caught sight of a redcoated soldier, walking purposefully up Fifth Street. She leaned forward to rest her forehead on the window glass, feeling her spirits sink. Thinking about Davey's secret, whatever it was, she had actually forgotten about the war for a few moments.

CHAPTER FOUR

The carriage rattled along Fourth Street. Mary sat next to her mother, the heavy woolen carriage robes tucked around her legs and waist, her pink shawl wrapped about her shoulders. Mary's mother touched her arm.

"I wanted you to accompany me so I might speak to you without someone overhearing."

Mary faced her mother.

"I know," her mother said. "I have never done this before. But you are no longer a child, Mary, and there are things you must begin to consider. I know that you think that you are too young to have an interest in these British officers. You are not."

Mary started to protest, but her mother silenced her by raising one gloved hand. "I would remind you that your father is nine years older than I am. I am not saying that you are ready for marriage. But the finest of England's young men are here, in our city, in our homes. This will never, never happen again. Any young man that you impress now . . ." She let her voice drop a little. "Mary, he could remember you, four or five years from now when he is looking for a wife. Or he may have a younger brother. One never knows."

Mary turned to look out the window again. She knew her mother was only trying to look to her future, but what if the war went on for another five years? What if William was killed—or the "young British officer" her mother kept talking about?

"Mary?"

"Yes?"

"Have you heard me? Choosing a husband is the single most important decision a young woman makes in her life. Everything else will be shaped by it."

Mary stared at her. "Don't you think about William?" It was barely a whisper and for a few seconds, Mary thought that her mother had not heard her. But she had.

"If you imagine that I forget my own son for even a minute, you insult me, Mary Alice Peale."

Samuel pulled the horses into a tight turn onto Union Street. As the coach swayed, Mary saw her mother's eyes glisten with tears. "What do you expect me to do? End the war? I wish I could. But all I can do—all any of us can do—is make the best of whatever comes to us in our lives. Your father did not want this war. Nor did I. Nor did any sensible subject of the king. But the rebels will not let well enough alone. They refuse to wait for the statesmen to settle matters."

Mary shook her head. "But even Father says the tea and stamp taxes are wrong."

"Yes. But rebellion is by far more wrong and in that opinion your father is unmovable. In matters of his honor he has always been so. It is one of the traits I admire in him. I wish . . ."

Mary waited for her mother to finish the sentence, but she did not. Instead, she raised her hand again, in the kind of fluid, graceful gesture that Abigale was beginning to learn. "Look there. What are they doing?"

Mary turned in the seat just as Samuel guided the team onto Front Street and urged them into a smart trot. As they got closer to Little Dock Street, Mary saw four British soldiers marching along, flanking two boys who looked thirteen or fourteen years old. The boys had halters fashioned from thick rope around their necks.

Mary looked at her mother, then back out the window. "Are they going to hang them?"

Her mother shook her head helplessly. "I hope not. But why else would they put the ropes around their necks like that?"

Mary shuddered as the bright red coats fell behind them and she could no longer see the pale, tense faces of the boys. For a few moments she and her mother rode without talking again, the hollow rhythm of the horses' hooves steady on the cobblestones. Then Samuel pulled the horses to a halt at the corner and Mary leaned out to look. A heavy brickyard wagon was crossing in front of them on Walnut Street, coming slowly up the rise from the landing. Samuel had pulled up as a courtesy to the horses, Mary knew, not the driver. It was hard for the animals to start off again uphill with such weight behind them if they had to stop. Samuel loved horses.

As they waited for the brick wagon to pass, Mary noticed two men arguing on the boardwalk in front of a tavern. She bent so that she could read the sign. THE MERRY CUTLER. The two men sounded anything but merry. Their voices were raised in anger. Mary could not help but hear what they were saying. One man stood with his back to her. He looked young, perhaps twenty. His dark hair was caught in a short ponytail, not powdered at all. He was speaking with his hands on his hips, his head tilted.

"I tell you they were drummer boys. Nothing more. They are not spies."

The other man, whose weathered face Mary could see clearly, grimaced as though he'd been struck. He shook his head. "But think, man! How can Provost Marshal Cunningham know that? They were part of Washington's army. They could have carried letters back with them."

The young man half turned and Mary could see the anger on his face before she heard it in his answer. "If you were going to recruit a spy, don't you imagine you would find one old enough to have the common sense to stay out of the streets in midday? Those boys were on their way to see their mothers."

The older man shrugged. "Drummer boys take the same chance as soldiers on the field of war. They should be treated the same by the law."

The younger man shook his head in exasperation. "This isn't the *law*." He gestured in the general direction of the redcoats a block or more away now. "This is a military occupation. A conquest, or a try at it. It's British interference in our affairs."

The carriage began to roll again as the older man shook his finger in his companion's face. "Every fool rebel in the city ought to be hanged," he was shouting. "If it wasn't for you damned upstarts, we'd have—"

"Can you read?" the younger man interrupted. "Thomas Paine's pamphlet *Common Sense* is forty-seven pages of plain thinking. Paine makes it clear that the ties with England are already torn beyond repair. He convinced me—"

"Convinced you to betray your king? Then he is a traitor, this Paine." The older man was nearly shouting, but his voice could not carry far enough for Mary to hear any more of what he said. She leaned back against the seat and watched the shop fronts on Second Street go past the window. She saw other groups of men talking, but couldn't hear any more than bits and pieces of what was being said.

Mary realized abruptly that her mother was looking at her, frowning. "It is not proper for you to be so interested in the affairs of men."

"It's hardly the men alone who are affected," Mary answered without thinking. For a second, her mother looked angry, then she smoothed her face and nodded without speaking, averting her eyes.

"I only want to hear what happened in Germantown," Mary said very quietly, watching her mother's profile. "I think William must have been there." Her mother nodded again but said nothing and stared out her own window, her face unreadable.

When Samuel pulled the horses to a stop, Mary's mother reached to straighten Mary's shawl. "There. You must begin to think of your appearance more often." Her voice was tight, but her manner was pointedly calm and cheerful, as though nothing unusual had been said between them, as though nothing more important than a day's outing was at hand.

Samuel opened the carriage door and offered Mary his arm. She leaned on him as she stood on the foot peg, then allowed him to lift her to the ground. She stood beside the carriage, looking over the pocked iron wheel rim at the street, as Samuel helped her mother down. Once they were both safely out of the carriage, Mary's mother cleared her throat. Samuel stood at attention before her. "Madam?"

"Wait here. I don't think we will be more than a few moments."

Samuel nodded. "Yes, madam."

Mary followed her mother up the boardwalk. Six British soldiers passed them going in the other direction. Mary ducked her head as they went by. As soon as they were far enough away, her mother turned and cupped Mary's chin in her hand. "Mary. Lift your head, walk proudly. Stays cannot correct a poor posture entirely."

Mary nodded obediently. She did not want to argue with her mother. But she did not want to attract the attentions of a British officer, either. Her mother waited until Mary's gaze met her own. "Remember what I told you. The war will end, one way or another. And then you will have the rest of your life to think about. God willing, so will William."

Mary lowered her eyes.

"Let us make haste, Mary," her mother said in a cheerful voice. "We cannot be at this all morning long. There is too much to be done back at Peale House." Mary followed her mother along the boardwalk, then up the front steps of the peruke maker's shop.

Inside, Mary walked in a slow circle, looking at the wigs resting on their wooden stands while her mother spoke to the proprietor. Some of the wigs were unbelievably complicated, rising so high off the stands with their rows of tight curls that it was hard to imagine anyone being able to wear one without feeling unbalanced.

"Not many wear those anymore," the wig maker said as he waited for his assistant to return with Mary's father's wig.

Mary's mother nodded. "One sees fewer and fewer of them now. A lot of the younger men powder their own hair."

The peruke maker shook his head. "That will pass. They will realize that all of Europe looks on them as crude and unfashionable."

Mary's mother nodded again in agreement. "It's just all this . . ." She waved her hands delicately.

"The war will pass," the wig maker responded. "No gentleman can be truly well dressed without a proper wig."

A little blond boy, still young enough to wear a dress, came wandering out of the back of the shop. The peruke maker picked him up and kissed him. A moment later, his wife appeared, apologizing for the intrusion.

"A pretty child," Mary's mother said.

The peruke maker nodded. "And sweet-natured. But if we leave the door open for an instant, he's through it and into the shop. If he lives, he'll be a traveler, I'd wager."

Mary's mother smiled at the jest. The assistant

reappeared, carrying a stiff box of brown paper that he handed to Mary.

"Cleaned, relined, and trimmed," the peruke maker said, writing out a receipt. "It will need redressing in six months or so. The pomade will dry."

Mary's mother took coins out of a little embroidered pocket bag that she pulled from her waistband.

"I thank you for your custom, madam," the peruke maker said, bowing slightly at the waist. His assistant had disappeared. He was probably busy in the back of the shop. He had the same round, dark eyes as the shop owner—perhaps he was a son, not a lad working out an indenture.

Mary's mother led the way back to the coach. Samuel took the box from Mary and secured it in the compartment behind the driver's bench. "Home, madam?"

"I want to go on to Combes Alley."

Samuel helped Mary back into the coach. She settled on the upholstered seat, sliding over to give her mother enough room for her panniered skirts. The coach lurched into motion and Mary caught at the leather handle set into the carriage top. She watched the endless row houses stream past. The brick looked impossibly red against the sky. "Do you think it will snow soon?"

Mary's mother shook her head. "God knows. I do not." She smiled.

At the chandler's, Mary waited while her mother bought three dozen molded bayberry candles. As she counted out the money, she turned to Mary. "Six for each parlor, and two dozen for the upstairs chandeliers. That way no one will end up with smelly tallow spattering their gowns."

As they came out the door, a sudden burst of shouting in the alley made Mary spin around, trying to see where it was coming from. "Calm yourself," her mother said sternly. "Raise your chin and act like a lady."

Mary was startled at her mother's tone of voice and obeyed without thinking. "I am sorry, Mary," her mother said after a moment of silence. "A woman's calmness is all she has. Her good temper and sweet nature are most important. Try to learn this."

Mary wanted to reach out and touch her mother's hand, to have her mother rock her the way she had done years ago when she was little. But she knew that was impossible. Nothing was the way it had been then.

CHAPTER FIVE

Mary ran upstairs. Her mother had disappeared into her father's office with the wig box. Now, if she could just avoid Abigale. On the landing, Mary slowed her step and walked as lightly as she could; she did not want to get trapped into talking about the ball or telling Abigale over and over that she would look beautiful in her gown. Mary reached up to straighten her little lace cap. How could anyone as pretty as her sister doubt her own beauty?

As Mary passed the workroom across from the ballroom she heard the tittering laughter of Florence and Emily over the clatter of the linen mangle. Just outside the door, a tray of unpolished silver awaited their attentions. Mary cleared her throat and the laughter hushed instantly. They were lucky it was she, not her mother or Abigale, who had heard them amusing themselves when they were supposed to be working. Her mother would have been angry and Abigale was beginning to act as if the household was her own to run. Mary could tell that sometimes it amused their mother, other times it annoyed her.

Mary opened the door to her room carefully and quietly. A sudden eruption of womanly laughter from Abigale's room startled her.

"We won't leave it like that, will we?" Abigale was asking.

More laughter. "Of course not, madam. The starch will only give it the height you want." The woman's voice was heavily accented with French pronunciation. Mary pulled her door closed very gently. She had forgotten. Abigale was with the hairdresser. It would no doubt take an hour or two. Perfect.

Mary sat carefully on the edge of her bed to change into her oldest pair of shoes—they were also her favorites. As she always did, she carefully switched them so that she would be wearing the one that had been on her left foot last time on her right foot this time. Her father said it would make them last longer.

As Mary struggled with her stays and petticoats, trying to reach the buckles, her bed creaked. The ropes that crisscrossed the frame needed waxing. The straw mattress on the bottom was matting down, too, getting hard as stone. It was time to tell her mother it needed replacing. Her feather mattress was still fine. The blue and white ticking cloth cover looked quite new. Mary loved the embroidery her mother had done along the borders.

On the opposite wall was Florence's bed. Mary often wished she could share her room with Rachel, or even silly Emily. But Rachel slept above the kitchen and Emily didn't live in Peale House. She walked back to her family's cottage in Quince Lane every evening. Mary felt a little guilty at her thoughts. Florence was not so bad. But she was boring—and she snored.

Mary stood and wriggled her toes to position her shoes. She lifted her petticoats, then let them fall. The carriage ride had flattened them a little. She didn't want her mother to notice. She didn't want anyone to stop her before she could get outside. Mary pulled her shawl close around her shoulders and tiptoed to the door. Her ear pressed against the smooth wood, she listened for a moment before she swung it open. The hinges were silent and she was grateful for her father's insistence that they be kept oiled all the time. He hated squeaking metal.

Mary pushed at the door, sliding her feet on the smooth pine planks, determined not to make a single sound. She turned toward the main stairway. She would just go to the kitchen and watch Rachel for a bit. Her mother would approve; she wanted Mary to learn about every aspect of the household. And if opportunity presented itself, she could scoot out the back door long enough to get a look inside the garden shed.

Mary went down the stairs quickly, turning into the wide entryway, then down the main hallway. Her stays were beginning to itch and pinch. Every evening, when she took off her corset, it was like a small piece of heaven to be able to scratch herself.

"Mistress Mary!" Rachel exclaimed when she came into the warming kitchen. "What brings you down here?"

Mary smiled, inhaling the rich scents of vanilla, butter, and sugar. The sugar loaf was sitting on the sideboard, unwrapped, the silver sugar knife lying next to it.

"Go ahead and cut yourself a tiny bit," Rachel said, following her glance.

"Only a little," Mary promised, pushing the knife against the sticky loaf. A thin slice curled away and she pinched it delicately between two fingers. The delicious sweetness melted in her mouth.

"Will you help me with the garden seed list?" Rachel asked. "Your father says he will let me order seeds on the next ship cargo he contracts. This time, he will ask the captain to bring them in his cabin and perhaps fewer will be ruined."

"I will write it for you." Mary glanced at the loaf of sugar, but knew her mother would get angry if she ate too much. Sugar was scarce now, because of the war. She walked away from the sideboard and looked into the great hearth. A bake kettle lay buried in glowing coals. It was the biggest kettle. Rachel was roasting a turkey, or perhaps a goose. A whole lamb was spitted and hung over the low burning fire on the left side of the hearth. Rachel reached forward and pulled on the crank, which turned the spit, then went back to her stirring. Mary peered into the open kettle, inhaling steam redolent of vanilla. The whitish mixture was simmering very slowly. Rachel had swung the black iron crane until the pot was over a log that had burned down to dull coals in a bed of white ash.

"Flummery!" Mary couldn't keep the excitement out of her voice. This was her father's favorite, next to syllabub.

"Flummery indeed," Rachel said, her eyes dancing. She loved it when people liked her cooking—which was most of the time. She had been their cook for as long as Mary could remember and no one had ever gotten sick at their table. And almost everyone pestered her mother for Rachel's receipts.

Mary bent over the pot and inhaled slowly. Rachel paused in her stirring just long enough to allow Mary to smell the pudding, then began the slow steady rhythm again.

"Yours is the best French flummery in Philadelphia, Rachel," Mary said, to earn one of the cook's grins.

"Thick and sweet, and like silk on the tongue," Rachel agreed. "It's because I use rose water and orange flower water, and because your father lets me purchase isinglass for Christmas and parties like this one. It's made from fish bladders."

Mary winced. "Fish?"

Rachel laughed aloud. "At least I don't have to make jelly from hart's horn or calves' hooves. And isinglass makes clearer jellies."

Mary watched Rachel stir. Her forearms were big, almost like a man's, from lifting the heavy iron pots and flour sacks and beating endless eggs into froth.

"I am going to cover the tray around it with brandied pears," Rachel said.

Mary nodded politely. "That will make a very pretty dish."

"I made a ribboned jelly."

Mary smiled. "May I see?"

Rachel nodded. "In the storeroom. You'd have seen it earlier except you were too busy watching the wood corders. I have two more layers to add."

Mary skipped through the storeroom door. It took her a moment to spot the jelly glasses. They were on a tray, set well back on the highest shelf. She pulled up the stool to get a better look. Rachel had opened the window farther to keep the storeroom cool enough to set the sweet dessert.

The jelly was beautiful. Rachel had used cochineal to color the bottommost layer deep red. Then came a layer the color of light chocolate, then one a pale green, probably colored with crushed mint. Those three layers were repeated again, then there was a thicker layer of yellowish cream.

"I'm going to finish it off with another green, then a nice thick layer of the cochineal," Rachel called.

"Mother will be so pleased," Mary said, stepping down off the stool. She glanced out the window. Davey was crossing the gardens. Was he coming into the house for more apples? Or going back to the garden shed? Mary watched him, standing far enough back from the window so he wouldn't be able to see her.

Davey hesitated when he got to the stone walk that led to the back door, turning to look at the garden shed. Just then Mary heard Samuel shout Davey's name. Davey jumped as though Samuel's voice had been a musket shot. He stood uncertainly for a second, before running back toward the carriage house. He took a path that carried him in a wide arc around the garden shed. Mary frowned, puzzled. What was Davey up to?

"Mistress Mary?" It was Florence's voice.

"Yes? I was just admiring Rachel's beautiful ribboned jellies." Mary came out of the storeroom and almost ran into Florence.

"Oh!" Florence put one hand over her heart. She was in her thirties, but sometimes she acted as though she were an old woman, fluttering her hands all the time and pressing her palm against her heart when anything upset her. "Mistress Abigale is looking for you. She asked me to send you up if I could find you."

Mary tried not to let her disappointment show.

"Thank you very much, Florence. I will be going up directly. Is her hair . . ." Mary paused. She shouldn't let Florence know that she didn't usually like the way Abigale's hair look dressed.

"Is Abigale still in her bedchamber?" Mary asked.

Florence nodded. "In front of the looking glass. She came to the door to summon me, then went back in."

Mary heard the disapproval in Florence's voice but she refused to take the bait and express her own. After a moment Florence began to move uneasily. Mary let her shift her weight from one foot to the other. Florence needed to be reminded that Mary wasn't a child who would not notice her tone of voice or the subtlety in what she said. "Abigale's gown is lovely, don't you think?" she asked finally. Florence nodded so eagerly that Mary felt guilty. Florence had been raised a Quaker and Mary knew that finery bothered her. Feeling ashamed of being such a bully, Mary dismissed Florence and watched her go out the kitchen door.

Mary hesitated at the doorway, thinking. This was probably her best chance to slip out to the garden shed. Her father was likely locked up with Benjamin, poring over his account books. Her mother would be preoccupied with the servants' preparations for tonight—and Abigale would be staring in a mirror, not looking out the window.

Rachel was busy at the hearth and did not turn as Mary left. A little breathless, Mary hurried out the back door, closing it silently behind herself. She paused on the little porch, looking out across the yard to make sure she was alone. Then she lifted her skirts and hurried down the steps.

The wood along the garden shed wall had been neatly stacked. That would please her father. Mary ducked around to the front of the shed—the door faced the stables—and leaned against the brick wall where the sun struck. It was wonderfully quiet. Mary felt deliciously warm and safe and alone. If anyone was looking from the windows now, they could not see her. She smiled. Unless someone had seen her run across the yard, or caught her going out the back door, no one would know she had left the house.

Mary smoothed her skirt and stooped to pick up a red leaf from the ground. The nights were getting cold. There would be snow soon. And her brother would be camping out in it somewhere, freezing and miserable, while British officers danced their evenings away with his sister, drinking his father's cider.

A rustling sound caught her attention and she

turned, squinting into the darkness behind the dusty little window. So. Davey did have some kind of creature in the shed. It sounded bigger than a kitten. Maybe it was a litter of kittens and they were playing together in the stacks of old newspapers and paper boxes her mother stored out here.

Mary stood away from the wall, breathing deeply and enjoying the mystery for a moment more. Once she knew what was in the shed, she would have to go back inside. It would not be long before someone was calling for her. Even though she couldn't see them, Mary felt the windows of Peale House looking down at her. She went to the shed door and turned the latch.

The interior of the shed was dark. It took her eyes a few seconds to adjust. Once they had, it took another few seconds for her mind to make sense out of what she was seeing. There were no kittens.

There, lying on the earthen floor, propped up by bloodied newspapers and an old blanket that Davey had probably stolen from the stable, was her brother.

CHAPTER SIX

"William?"

Mary whispered his name but he did not hear her. Or he could not. The front of his shirt was dark with dried blood. His right arm was in a crude sling fashioned from torn blue cloth and his eyes were closed.

Mary clung to the door handle, trying to still her thundering heart. How long had William been here? Since the battle? Or for a few hours? Why hadn't Davey told someone?

"Oh, William," Mary breathed. His skin was so white and he was so still. A sudden terror gripped her and she stepped into the shed and bent down. No. He was not dead. His hand was warm. But he did not stir at her touch.

Mary straightened and stepped back again, uncertain, wringing her hands and trying to think. What should she do? She pulled off her shawl and laid it over William, then went out. She closed the door behind herself, making sure the latch caught.

Mary ran across the yard to the back porch. She was through the door and halfway down the hall before she realized that she was heading toward her father's office. She slowed her step.

Perhaps she should tell her mother. But then her mother would likely tell her father anyway. And he might turn William out. He had said as much, hadn't he? Mary stood uneasily, looking up the hallway. Her heart ached. She had to do something. But what?

"Mistress Mary, there you are!" It was Florence, breathless, coming out of the warming kitchen. "Your mother says you are to watch Rachel finishing the syllabub."

Mary opened her mouth to protest but then pressed her lips together again. What could she say? She nodded distractedly and followed Florence into the kitchen. Her mother was standing near the hearth, looking at a haunch of venison that had been hung over the flames on a roasting hook.

"Mary, we've been looking up and down for you."

Mary nodded, avoiding her mother's questioning eyes. "Is that the syllabub?" she asked, to take the attention from herself. She pointed at a bowl of froth that Rachel was beating in circles, the heavy metal whisk a blur of motion.

Her mother nodded. "I wanted you to see the whole process. Rachel is quite extraordinary in regard to syllabubs. You will one day wish to instruct your own cook to do as well as she."

Mary nodded, barely hearing the words. Her mother smiled happily. She loved the kitchen, and was always giving Rachel new ideas to try.

"Rachel will tell you what she's done so far."

Rachel did not stop stirring, but she spoke, reciting the receipt she had used. "I take a quart and a half pint of thick cream, and a pint of Rhenish and a half pint of sack. Then three lemons and almost a pound of fine sugar. First I sift the sugar and mix it into the cream."

Mary's mother glanced at her and she nodded to show that she was listening, even though she knew she wasn't going to remember any of this later.

"You grate the rind off the three lemons. Then you put the grated rind and the juice into the Rhenish and sack." Rachel waited for Mary to nod, then she smiled broadly, still whipping the liquid in circles in the bowl. "Then you add all of that to the cream and whisk it half an hour. Use a silver spoon to fill your glasses." She smiled. "It will keep good nine or ten days."

Mary glanced up to find her mother staring at her. "Mary? Are you all right? You look pale."

Mary forced a smile. "I am fine, Mother."

Her mother crossed the room, scrutinizing her. "Did you take a chill while we were out in the carriage?" Mary shook her head again and took a step backward, but her mother was already reaching toward her, touching her forehead, then pressing one palm against Mary's cheek.

"Why, Mary, you are still quite cold."

"I was just out in the garden," Mary said quickly, then regretted it. Now her mother was looking at her even more closely.

"And why were you there?"

"I was looking for late onions. I thought Rachel might want to roast a few for garnish for . . . the lamb," Mary finished, her eye falling on the dark meat roasting over the fire. Her mother would approve, she knew, would even be pleased with her interest in the food for their guests.

"Mary, that is very thoughtful and would be good indeed. And did you find onions?"

Mary shook her head, looking back at the syllabub that was so white and frothy now that it looked like clouds in the deep china bowl. "No. No, I could not."

"But there are onions still in the ground. Parsnips, too," Florence said from the doorway. "Clear as daylight. Over in the very same corner where you watched me plant them last May, Mistress Mary."

Mary glanced at her, then at her mother. "Well. I suppose I didn't look as well as I might have," she began.

"Must not have looked at all," Florence jibed, smiling. The smile withered under a look from Mary's mother.

"It was chilly out," Mary said, defending herself. She felt like screaming at Florence. What difference did it make about the onions? Florence just loved to be *right* about things.

Mary's mother was looking at her again, that searching stare that made Mary want to turn her head away. She forced herself to smile instead. "I am perhaps a little tired, Mother."

Her mother nodded, watching her.

"I may go up and try to nap a little before the guests come."

"They will begin arriving at four o'clock, Mary.

You have a little over an hour and a half."

Mary nodded, feeling breathless and frightened. Maybe she should just tell her mother about William. Her mother would call for a doctor and bring him into the house. Or would she? Her father would be the one to decide, not her mother, and Mary knew it. "I believe . . ." she began, without really knowing what she was going to say. "I believe I will just go upstairs and lie down a bit."

"You could bring in the onions first," her mother said. "It is well to finish what you start. Run and get your pink shawl if it was too chilly without it."

Mary smiled, locking her hands together to keep herself from wringing them again. "I think I will be warm enough this time." She waved one hand at the hearth, the steamy windows, Rachel's still-whirling syllabub. The whisk made a sound like water rushing over stones. "I am so very warm now. All the way through."

Mary's mother turned to the door, making a shooing motion with her hands. "Quickly, then. Or you won't have time for your nap."

Mary walked, stiff-legged and nervous, toward the door. What she really wanted to do was run upstairs and get blankets from the linen storage, or even her old blue shawl—why hadn't she thought of that? Why had she said she didn't need one? She glanced back. Her mother was talking to Rachel, but Florence was still watching her. Abruptly, Mary's mother turned from Rachel. "Florence? The candlesticks are polished? And the fruit trays? Have you thought of the candle snuffers?"

Florence's low voice faded behind Mary as she went out of the kitchen and turned toward the back door. She would get the onions, quickly; then, once she was sure no one was watching for her, she would take blankets to William. Maybe Samuel and Davey would help her. They could take William to a doctor and help find him somewhere safer to stay. He couldn't stay where he was now. At four o'clock there would be dozens of British officers arriving. They would be walking the grounds all evening long, flirting and drinking and dancing.

Mary went out the back door, deliberately walking at a normal pace in spite of her racing thoughts. The yard seemed unreal to her, like a painting. Along the fence, the pear trees had dropped their leaves. They looked like rough brown chandeliers, turned upside down. The vegetable rows were mostly barren now—Rachel used their own vegetables as much as she could. The weather had been cold enough so that the outer leaves of the lettuce and the tops of the celeriac had browned a little. The broccoli had long since been cut, and the bean vines rattled their drying pods in the breeze. A dozen cabbages still stood shoulder to shoulder in their row.

Mary glanced at the garden shed. Shivering with worry and confusion, she tried to remember where Florence had planted the onions. May seemed a lifetime ago. Finally she saw them, still green topped, in the corner of the garden closest to the stables.

Mary pulled four of the biggest onions, shaking the cold, dry soil from the little fan of roots at the base of the bulbs. Then she glanced at the house. Careful that she did not look as suspicious as Davey had earlier, Mary crossed the yard, carrying her onions. She set them on the porch, then turned as if she were going to get more. But instead of stopping in the garden, she kept walking, her head high, as though she had just decided to go to the stables on a sudden whim. If her mother happened to look out the window, she might get angry, but she wouldn't think anything was amiss. Mary could tell her that she wanted to see the new gelding that Davey had talked about.

Mary hurried into the arching doorway of the carriage house first, hoping that Davey and Samuel would be sitting near the little hearth, polishing a harness or mending it. But neither was there. Telling herself that they had to be close by, she went through the wide door used to bring the horses from their stalls.

"David? Samuel?" Mary called, her eyes adjusting to the dim, hay-sweet interior. The new gelding whinnied a challenge. No human voice answered. The matched mares were probably out in their paddock on the side of the stables that faced Fifth Street. Mary called twice more before going back out into the carriage house. She stood at the foot of the ladder that led up to the hayloft where Davey slept, then glanced behind herself. The door to the small room that held Samuel's cot and trunk was closed. She called again, but there was no answer. Only then did it occur to her to look back into the carriage room. The dark green town carriage was there, the bright oaken shafts propped on a wooden stand, but the little open brougham was gone. Her mother, or perhaps her father, had sent David and Samuel on some errand.

Mary fought tears. *Now* what could she do? Trying not to cry, Mary ran back across the yard and up the steps, refusing to look at the garden shed as she passed it.

The kitchen seemed impossibly hot and steamy after the crisp outdoor air. Grateful that her mother had gone about some other work, Mary gave Rachel the onions. Rachel smiled. "Thank you, mistress. I'll cut them to look like white roses."

"Tell Mother," Mary began softly, then cleared her throat. "If you see Mother tell her I will be resting upstairs until time to dress."

Rachel set the onions on the sideboard. "I will, mistress."

In the hallway, Mary heard men's voices in the front parlor. She hurried across the entry to the stairs and went up, then stopped on the landing, where she could hear without being seen.

"I'll tell them to bring them around. Just the two." It was a voice she didn't recognize. Then her father spoke.

"That will be fine. We'll just put them upstairs. The third floor will be best, above the noise and whatnot. No one uses the third-floor bedchambers now. The three eldest have married and gone."

"His Majesty appreciates the help of every loyal subject, sir."

"I am entirely happy to provide the rooms and what care we can." Mary's father's voice was a little louder, clearer. Footsteps sounded on the wood floor below and Mary drew back against the wall as she heard the parlor door open. Her father would probably walk his visitor to the front door now.

Mary ran lightly up six or seven more steps, then paused again. She and her sisters had always listened to the workings of the household from the stairs. No one below could look up and see them, and anyone coming suddenly from above could be fooled into thinking the listener was just on her way up. Mary stood with one foot on the step above. Becky had showed her the trick one gloomy, boring, winter's day.

"Good day to you," the unfamiliar voice was saying. "The men will bring the stretchers round."

"We shall ready the rooms," Mary heard her father answer. She moved a half step toward the railing and caught a flash of red over the top of the banister just as the front door opened. It was a British officer. Mary's father cleared his throat and she started, moving back from the railing again. The front door closed.

After Mary heard her father's footsteps fade down the wide hallway, she turned and went up the second flight of stairs. Her hands were sweating. So. They were going to bring two of the British wounded here? There would be two strangers lying in the little third-story room that had been her bedroom, shared with Abigale, when they were little. Mary clenched her fists. Two strangers lying in their soft beds while her own brother lay on a dirt floor in a cold garden shed.

CHAPTER SEVEN

Mary paced the length of her room, trying to think, to decide what she should do. Florence had laid her gown carefully across the foot of her bed. Abigale would be lying down now, Mary thought, with cold compresses on her face and bosom, to put roses in her skin. Mary stopped pacing and stood very still for a moment, fighting a second rush of tears. Voices in the hall startled her, and she went to stand close to her door, listening.

"Hurry, then," Florence was saying. A second or two later, Mary heard the door to the third-story stairs being opened and her mother's voice.

"Quick now, Emily. Throw open the window in the old bedchamber and build the fire. Then close it up again to keep in the warmth. Emily? When you've finished with the fire, shake out the linens, and Florence can give the floors a quick wash. Hurry!"

Mary could hear footsteps as the women climbed the steep stairs. Her mother called back down to the first floor, "Can you have them wait just a few moments please, sir?"

An unfamiliar voice assented, then all was silent for a full minute or two. Time crept by. Mary pressed her ear against her door.

"Mother?"

That was Abigale's voice, petulant and sleepy. Mary heard her sister's door close. "Mother?"

A heavy clumping on the narrow stairs preceded Florence's answer. "Your mother is downstairs, mistress. They've brought us two of the wounded from Germantown, found just this morning, poor fellows, lying in some ditch. All the beds in Philadelphia are filling up, I suppose. We must all do our part."

"Thank you, Florence, for the explanation," Abigale said, and Mary could hear the disdain in her voice. Sometimes Florence's little lectures were annoying, but Abigale was being rude.

Mary pressed her ear against her door, wishing she had never come upstairs. Now she was trapped. She should have stayed in the kitchen. Then, at least, she could have slipped out the back door when she heard Samuel and Davey return.

"Mary?" There was a sharp knock on her door. Mary sprang back, startled, her pulse hard and quick. She tried to look only mildly surprised as she opened the door.

"Are you resting well with all this noise?" Abigale's voice was edged with sarcasm. Her hair had been piled on top of her head, a dramatic cascade of curls falling down over one shoulder. She had left it dark, natural; it had not been powdered. She looked lovely except for the irritation in her expression.

"They can hardly help it, Abigale." Mary gestured toward the open stairway door. "They are readying it for two of the battle wounded."

Abigale nodded. "So I was told. By Florence."

Mary stared at her sister. She wasn't quite awake—but even so, there was no excuse for her unpleasant, unladylike manner. Florence was walking past, her eyes fixed upon the floor. She had obviously heard her name and was wary of any exchange with Abigale. Abigale watched her go by without saying anything until Florence was clumping her way up the narrow stairs with her fresh rags and wash bucket.

"I do hope they can get them settled quickly. How are we supposed to ready ourselves with strangers walking up and down the hall?"

Mary shook her head again. Abigale wouldn't be acting like this if she knew William was hurt, too. Emily came past, carrying an armload of kindling and a lit candle. Mary waited until she was gone, then looked up and down the hall. For the moment, they were alone. "Abigale? In the garden shed—" she began.

"Where is Mother?" Abigale interrupted her. "Does she know about this?"

"Of course," Mary said. "She was here a few minutes ago. Abigale, listen . . ."

Florence came huffing back down the stairs, her bucket full of dark water now. "The floor is finished." She said it on her way past, without looking at Abigale or Mary. Abigale yawned. Mary took a quick breath and tried once more.

"Abigale, I need to talk to you."

Abigale looked at her with sudden interest. "Why? You aren't going to try to hide in your room tonight, are you? Because Mother won't allow it, Mary."

Mary tried to start over, to tell Abigale about

William, but it was too late. Their mother's voice came up from below. "Florence, get the doors open, please. Then run up and warn the girls that they are coming. Did you move the trunks and the old cradle to one side up there? Pull down the hallway clothesline that Emily strung up there during the last rainstorm, too."

Mary and Abigale turned together, facing the stairs. They watched Florence approach at a run, her face pink. "The men are coming," she said in passing them, and went straight up the narrow stairs. Then Abigale seemed to realize that she was still wearing only her dressing gown. She hurried back to her own room. Mary stood, transfixed, as the cadence of boots came up the stairs.

The first man was lying on a stretcher, his eyes closed as his bearers carried him. The second bearer held his end high to keep the stretcher level on the stairs. The other wounded man was walking, with the help of a redcoated officer. His thigh and one arm were heavily bandaged. His face contorted with pain, he tried to give a polite greeting to Mary. He could not master his voice and made only a low sound in his throat. Mary stared at him. His bandages had been freshly changed, his shirt was clean. The man supporting him smiled. "Your parents are very kind to let these two stay here."

Mary nodded uncomfortably. "I hope they recover," she managed, surprised to find that she meant it. She did not wish these men ill, not even if one of them was the one who had hurt William. The idea of musket fire or cannon shot tearing *any* man apart made her sad and angry and queasy all at once.

The officer seemed to read her thought. "You have to wonder what's worth it, don't you? Is anything?"

Mary watched as he guided his charge through the doorway, just as Florence came pattering back down. They struggled past each other and Florence fled down the hall toward the stairs without looking at Mary.

The officer tried to help the wounded man climb the first few steps, then gave up, calling out to the stretcher bearer. "He's going to have trouble here, Henry. Perhaps with two of us . . ."

A staccato of boot heels on the stairs announced the stretcher bearer's arrival. "I'll get on the other side, then, Dr. Morris," Henry said in a broad London accent.

Mary felt her heart stop, then start again. *Doctor?* She stood, unable to move or speak, staring at the men as they disappeared up the steep stairs. A muted collection of thumps and bangs signaled their arrival on the floor above. Voices filtered back down the stairs. Mary heard one of the wounded men cry out in pain. Had they moved the man on the stretcher to one of the beds?

Mary stood still. The officer was a doctor. Could she get him to look at William? Would he? He had hundreds of British soldiers to tend, didn't he? And he was British, part of George III's regular army; a professional soldier.

Mary heard boot heels on the stairs. The officer came out first, the two stretcher bearers just behind him. "Miss?"

"Sir?" Mary's voice was trembling and she could not stop it.

"Could you tell your mother that I will be back in about a half hour? We are going to go find a bit of supper, but then we are going to—"

"Mary?"

It was Abigale, coming out of her room, wearing not her new emerald gown but her next best, a very flattering dress of deep blue. Mary heard the doctor pull in a breath, and she looked at him for the first time. He wasn't very old and he was good-looking, with dark hair and eyes.

"I hope you gentlemen are being helped in every possible way," Abigale said, gliding toward them. She smiled at the doctor and he smiled back at her.

"I was just asking your sister to let your mother know that we will be back soon. The bandages will need changing once more tonight, and I was going to see if Heacock would take a little broth. I don't think Thomas will be able to sup, but Heacock might."

"I am sure that supper for you and broth for the wounded men can be found in the Peale House kitchen, Major . . ." Abigale let her voice soften in a pause, leaving a little space for him to fill with his name. He obliged her.

"Dr. Richard Morris, Miss . . ." He left a similar void and Abigale smiled.

"Abigale. Abigale Peale. Welcome to Peale House, Dr. Richard Morris."

Abigale fell into step beside the doctor. The two stretcher bearers went ahead, glancing back once or twice to look appreciatively at Abigale. At the foot of the stairs, Mary's father met them, looking at Abigale with a fleeting smile. "Well, I see you have met my daughters, Dr. Morris."

The officer smiled and nodded. "I have indeed, kind sir. And I most appreciate their help and hospitality."

"I told him that Peale House could surely provide supper for him and broth for his patient," Abigale said.

"Of course," Mary's father said without hesitation. "You happen to find us on the brink of a night of entertainment. Perhaps you would join us, sir?"

Dr. Morris seemed to hesitate, but he nodded, smiling for an instant at Abigale. As soon as he had accepted the invitation, Abigale made a polite excuse about needing to get dressed for the ball and she turned and started back toward her room, ascending with little graceful steps that made her hair bounce. She did not look back. Understanding that the invitation was not meant for them, the two soldiers went out the front door, calling pleasantries to the doctor as they left.

"I fully understand if your daughter's kind impulse is not agreeable to your wife or yourself," Dr. Morris was saying.

"We are honored to help the king's soldiers," Mary's father said, steering the doctor across the entryway, then under the arched doorway and down the main hallway toward the kitchen. He lifted his voice. "Rachel? Rachel, we have a hungry soldier here." Mary trailed after them.

Mary's father leaned down to whisper in her ear as the doctor went into the kitchen. "There's no reason for you to stay, Mary. You should go get dressed. Florence will be up to help you both soon, I am sure."

Mary nodded helplessly, looking toward the back door. "Is Davey back yet?" she asked her father. He glanced at the doctor. Rachel had seated him at a small table and was asking him his preferences.

"Yes. I asked him and Samuel to go get a fresh roll of painted canvas flooring. Your mother thought to protect the entry from tonight's inevitable mud and sand. She found last year's canvas was mildewed when Florence and Emily brought it down."

Mary nodded absently. Last winter's canvas had been painted to look like black-and-white squares of marble. Mary looked past her father toward the back door again.

"Did I bring in enough onions?" she asked Rachel suddenly. Rachel smiled and nodded. "I could surely go to fetch more if you had not, mistress."

Mary sensed her father watching her. She knew he wanted her to go, probably so he could get the doctor to talk about the Germantown battle. She looked once more toward the garden. While they were in the kitchen, she decided, she would get blankets out of the linen storage. She could at least make sure that William was warm enough. Maybe he would be awake now and he could tell her what to do. Even if he wasn't, perhaps she could ask Davey to keep checking on William. It would be easier for him to get away than for her. Mary frowned. Why hadn't Davey told someone? Maybe he was afraid her father would get angry if he helped William.

Mary clenched her fists. Of course. Davey would not want to get involved. His contract was for four more years. Her father could sell it to anyone—a shopkeeper, a tanner, a ship's captain. Davey was very happy in the stable with Samuel, learning about the horses. Maybe he wouldn't help.

Mary laid her heavy thoughts aside and went down the hall, listening for voices ahead of her. At the arched entryway door, Florence passed her, bustling toward the kitchen carrying a silver tray stacked with plateware and pewter from the front parlor. As she topped the stairs, Mary could hear her mother scolding Emily.

"I have instructed you both to rub the pewter and Britannia with oiled flannel for the spots. *First*. Then you must wash it in soap and water and then *dry* it before you use the whiting and sweet oil. Only the silver gets the rottenstone and sweet oil before anything else."

Mary felt sorry for Emily and Florence. Apparently their giggling had kept them from doing an adequate job. Mary slipped past the workroom and turned the corner, stopping at the first small door on her right.

Mary opened the storage closet and took out two of their oldest blankets, thick woolen ones with bound edges, from beneath the newer, better ones on the back shelf. Carrying them against her chest, she peeked out into the still, empty hall, then bolted. She nearly ran, knowing that there would be no way to explain away the blankets in her arms if her mother saw her.

As she passed back by the workroom, Mary could hear the silver-polishing lecture continuing, and the small apologetic sounds that Emily was making. She went down the wide stairs, feeling sorry for her. Emily was cheerful and nice and she lived with her widowed mother and supported her. She had no brothers, no other kin at all, and would have to care for her mother until the old woman died. She would likely be too old to marry by the time she was free to do so.

Halfway down the wide hall Mary could hear her father, his voice muffled by the walls. She could hear the doctor's response as she got close to the kitchen door.

"It was probably foolish of Washington to try so complicated a strategy with such untrained troops." Mary's father made a sound of assent.

"But it's all foolish," the doctor went on. "Anyone who has seen the men dying, torn to pieces, has to question war altogether. Neither side really wins, sir."

Mary slowed her step, listening, looking nervously behind herself. The instant that her father began to speak she darted past the doorway, glancing in to see Rachel busily working beside the hearth, using the bread peel to loosen a pastry on a flat tin sheet. The doctor and her father were at the sideboard. The doctor sounded as if he hated war as much as she did. Maybe he *would* help William if she asked him.

The back door latch made a little creak as Mary pulled it down, but the hinges were silent. She stepped down onto the chilly porch. The sunshine was fading. It was getting cold. Guests would be arriving soon.

Mary ran without glancing up at the windows desperate to see William. All her fears pushed forward, crowding her thoughts. What if he had died while she was gone? It would be her fault for not telling. Instead of helping him, she would be responsible for his death. Her heart constricted at the thought.

Mary shifted the heavy blankets into one arm,

freeing her right hand for the garden shed door. She pressed the latch and fumbled clumsily for a moment, then opened the door slowly, afraid of what she would see. As the pale sunlight leapt into the dark interior of the shed, Mary let out a tiny scream and dropped the blankets onto the cold ground. The shed was empty.

CHAPTER EIGHT

For a few seconds, Mary could only stare at the scuffed dirt floor. Then she looked wildly around the yard. Had William managed to stand, then? Maybe he was all right. Maybe the blood had been someone else's, or his wound had bled a lot, but was not serious. But then where was he? Mary began to tremble.

"*Sssssst.*"

The little sound startled Mary and she whirled around, half expecting William to be standing there, dirty and hurt. But there was no one.

"*Ssssssst.*"

This time she was certain of the direction the noise had come from. But she still couldn't see anything. She stared at the withered garden and the pear trees beyond it.

"*Ssst.*" The noise was smaller this time. Just enough to direct her eye. Davey was standing among the pear trees, his thin face framed by the bare twigs. Mary glanced around herself, then back at Davey. As soon as she moved away from the shed, she would be plainly visible from any of the windows on this side of the house. She turned back and laid the blankets just inside the shed door, then latched it shut. Then she picked up her skirts and, trying to look as though nothing was wrong, made her way across the withered garden and pretended to look at the remaining cabbages.

"I took your shawl, mistress," Davey said. "Couldn't just leave it there."

Mary nodded. "Of course. Where is he?"

Davey jutted his chin toward the carriage house. "Up in the loft where I sleep. Back behind the hay."

Mary nodded again. "There's a doctor in the kitchen. A British officer. He's talking to Father."

"William says he won't see a doctor. He says if he can get well, then he just will, without help."

Mary stood straight and faced him. "He talked? He's all right then?"

Davey shook his head. "He talked. He isn't well, Mistress Mary. You must have seen all the blood."

She nodded. "I want to see him."

Davey gestured. "Walk this side of the yard, through the trees. Less chance of anyone seeing."

Mary followed him as he led the way. She held her skirts close, but even so, the pear twigs seemed to grab at her skirt, pulling and snagging.

Once they reached the side wall of the carriage house, Davey gestured and she went first, hurrying, ducking into the wide doors. Davey was right behind her. "Can you manage the ladder?"

Mary nodded. "I will."

Davey followed her. She fought the fullness of her skirts and the restrictive pressure of her stays, but she managed to climb the ladder and stepped into the loft. "William?" She could not see anything clearly; the loft had no window. "William?"

"Here." The single word held so much pain that Mary caught her breath. Then Davey had her arm and was steering her to the back of the loft. She stumbled in the loose hay, but Davey kept her from falling.

William was lying near the eave, propped up by

a mound of hay. Her shawl was wrapped about him.

"Oh, William," Mary breathed. "I brought you blankets, but I—"

"Don't tell them."

Mary shook her head. "I haven't, but—"

"Promise me. Swear it, Mary."

Mary sank down onto the hay next to him. "I promise. But William, you need a doctor."

"No."

Mary glanced back over her shoulder at Davey. He shrugged and whispered. "That is what he's said since I found him this morning. He won't let me do anything. He barely let me talk him into moving up here. But I thought tonight, with all the couples . . ." He trailed off and Mary knew he was afraid she would be angry at what his words implied about Abigale. But it was true. Once the ball began, there was no way to know who would come walking in the yard, looking for a place with enough privacy for serious courtship and stolen kisses.

"You were right to bring him here, Davey."

"The ladder . . ." William said, then he stopped, taking in a jagged breath. "Almost killed me." He laughed a little, then coughed again.

Davey grimaced, looking at Mary. "Samuel doesn't know that he's up here yet. But he will have to soon."

"No."

"William!" Mary exploded. "You have to let someone help you. Maybe Samuel would know what to do. We should tell him now. He dresses wounds on the horses and he—"

A choking sound from William brought Mary up short. For a few seconds, terror gripped her heart, then she realized he was laughing.

"Mary, you flatter me," he managed and she smiled, realizing what she had said.

"I only meant he might know what to do."

William drew in another painful breath. "I know. What you meant. But I don't want to endanger him, too. I didn't intend to come here." Mary waited while he took two more breaths, then he went on. "I suppose I was too hurt to think clearly, but just able to walk. I remember the musket fire and Hudson shouting at me to get down. I remember falling. I got here somehow." He fell silent, as though so many words at once had exhausted him.

Mary felt Davey's hand on her shoulder. "Samuel's coming. I hear the brougham. Your mother had him out on one last errand. More brandy was needed, I think."

"Go now," William rasped.

Mary stood up, staring at her brother.

"Go."

Mary turned and struggled through the ankle-deep hay, then let Davey help her back down the ladder. She was standing in front of the new gelding's stall when Samuel turned into the carriage house, the clatter-grind of the iron-rimmed wheels coming to a halt as he reined in the mares. He doffed his hat and saluted her politely. She smiled back at him.

"Get those blankets out of the garden shed for William as quickly as you can," she said to Davey as they walked out together. "It's getting colder."

"Davey? Unhitch." Samuel's curtness reflected his own irritation, Mary was sure. Why should Davey be chatting while he had to chase about on last-minute errands?

"Don't tell him about William," Mary whispered to Davey.

He nodded, accepting her authority to decide. Then he shrugged. "He doesn't want me to. I won't if you say not to."

Mary glanced back up toward the hayloft. "Don't tell. We should do what William wants us to do. Except this much. If I think I can trust that British doctor, I am going to ask him to look at William out here. I will throw a pebble on the roof to warn you if we come." Davey nodded.

"Davey?" Samuel's voice was tight, impatient.

Mary turned to go. "Don't forget the blankets. As soon as you can."

Davey glanced at the garden shed. "I won't."

Mary felt as if she should say something more. But Samuel was waiting and she did not want him angry at Davey and watching him closely. Mary was coming back through the gardens when she heard her mother's voice from the porch.

"Mary! Whatever are you about?"

She started, nearly stumbling. "I was just . . . I just . . ." She gestured vaguely at Peale House as she neared the porch. "I was waiting for the soldiers to be settled before I dressed," she managed.

Her mother looked at her, her eyes softening. "It is strange to help them and then to think about William, isn't it?"

"Madam?" Rachel looked out the back door.

Mary's mother turned. "Yes, Rachel?"

"All is ready."

"You are a marvel and a wonder, Rachel," Mary's mother said warmly. Rachel beamed. "The distractions you've had today, I cannot imagine how you finished on time."

Rachel smoothed her apron. It was spotted with grease, and ashes had grayed the hemline. "I suppose I should change aprons."

"It's time we all dressed," Mary's mother said,

herding Mary gently up the stairs and through the back door. "There is little time left even if everyone is fashionably late." She smiled, reaching around Mary to pull the door closed. "I've had Florence take basins of warm water up for your baths, and she's laid out your gown and Abigale's. Abigale is dressing now." She faced Mary, looking into her eyes. "Try to have a good time this evening, Mary. There's nothing we can do about poor dear William or any of the rest of this." She spread her graceful hands out to indicate the war, the wounded, the king, George Washington, the world of politics, and men's affairs.

Mary glanced past her mother toward the back door as they passed into the hall. Her mother squeezed her shoulders and turned her around. "Go and bathe and dress. Florence will be up to help you and Abigale with your stays."

Mary hesitated. A loud knocking on the front door resounded through the house. Mary's mother made a little sound of dismay. "Florence? Florence!" The servant appeared, her cheeks still rosy with agitation. "Let our guests into the front parlor and tell them we will be with them shortly." Florence spun around and ran to obey. "Oh!" Mary's mother said. "I must rush now, too. I do hope your father is dressed. He would still be talking that doctor to death if I hadn't interrupted them." She gave Mary a little push. "Wait until Florence has them in the parlor. Then *run*."

With that, she was gone, checking one last time to see that Rachel had attended to everything. Mary knew that if she was still standing in the hallway when her mother came out of the kitchen she would be in for a scolding. She watched from the unlit center of the hallway as Florence led several redcoated officers, two with sparkling young women on their arms, into the parlor. Then she hurried across the entry and dashed up the stairs.

The basin of bath water was almost cool when Mary dipped her fingers into it. There was a little lump of hard lavender soap and two linen cloths beside it on the dresser. Mary wet one cloth and rubbed a little soap into it. She washed her face and neck thoroughly, making sure that her ears were clean. Then she scrubbed at her hands and forearms. Wringing the soap out and rinsing the cloth, she went over her skin again. Finished with her bath, she dried herself with the second cloth.

Mary went to her clothespress and took out a fresh chemise and her best stays. A moment later, Florence tapped on the door and came in, still out of breath. Without wasting words she undid Mary's everyday stays and helped her into her best. She pulled the laces tight so abruptly that Mary squeaked.

"I apologize, mistress. I am just in such an awful hurry."

"No matter," Mary said quickly, squirming to make the corset pinch less.

"Shall I help you with the rest, Mistress Mary?"

Mary looked at the watteau and its quilted petticoat. It was slightly out of style, of course. That was why her mother had had it cut down for her. "I think I can manage," she said. "But come back after Abigale for just a minute, please. For my hair and shoes."

"Yes, mistress," Florence said on her way out.

Mary managed her petticoat and the yellow silk overdress. She arranged the sleeves, pinning the fabric in three or four places to make it drape correctly. Then she sat on the edge of her bed and tried again to wriggle the stays into some semblance of comfort, but it was impossible. Mary stood up and walked to her clothespress. Bending at the knees, she picked up her yellow silk slippers. These, too, had been her mother's. Her feet had grown so in the past year that they fit without any paper wadding at all. She set them on her bed just as Florence tapped on her door and came in.

"Mistress Abigale was nearly ready all on her own," Florence panted. "Her hair is done, of course, and she had her shoes on, and her chemise. All I had to do was lace her stays, then lift the gown over her head."

Mary teetered on one foot as Florence slipped on one shoe, then the other. Florence went to the dressing table and brought back her brush. "You are so fortunate," Florence said as she went to work. "God has curled yours."

Mary stood still, her mind awash in uneasiness and conflict. Dr. Morris sounded as if he hated war—but what if he turned William over to the British provost marshal? If they had hanged those boys she had seen from the carriage window, what would they do to a real Continental soldier?

"Let me get the ribbons in, now," Florence said, using both hands to straighten Mary's head. "Don't move." Mary realized she hadn't noticed whether her mother's hair had been freshly arranged or not. Maybe she was going to wear a wig.

"There!" Florence stood back. "In another two or three years, you'll be the beauty they are all talking about."

Mary blushed. "I hardly think so, Florence. But thank you for doing my hair. I am sure it looks nice."

"There's a lot to be said for a warm heart. It shines through a girl's eyes," Florence said. Mary blushed again. She knew that Florence was thanking her for chiding Abigale's rudeness, but it made her feel awkward to be complimented for it.

"Are you ready, daughters?" Her father's voice came from the hallway.

Mary took a deep breath. "I am, Father," she called back. She heard Abigale say something but couldn't understand her words.

Florence opened the door. "I'll just be going back to the kitchen, then, mistress," she said over her shoulder. She lowered her eyes and went out, leaving the door standing open.

Mary's father smiled in at her. His breeches were of stone-colored silk, the silver buckles at the knees polished and glinting in the candlelight. "You look very pretty, Mary." She curtsied and he smiled wider.

Abigale's door opened. Rustling with silk, she came into the hall. Her hair perfectly accented the long curve of her neck. Her skin was delicate pink, roses pinched into her beautiful cheeks. Mary watched her father straighten with pride. "You look like a painting, Abigale. A Greek goddess." He was absolutely sincere. His face creased into a smile. There was so much love and pride in his eyes that

Mary stared. How could he be the same father who had disowned William?

He offered Mary his left arm and Abigale his right. Together they descended the stairs and made their way across the entry hall, their footsteps muted on the painted canvas carpet. Mary looked up from the marble pattern to see that the double doors of the front parlor had been flung open, revealing the interior, polished and dramatic beneath the flicker of the wall sconce candles.

As they entered the room, conversation stopped. Florence had pulled the chairs away from the walls and arranged them in a formal semicircle, stretching away from the left side of the blazing fireplace, then curving back around to its right. The mahogany tables shone like mirrors and the pier glass reflected the hearth candles and the glittering gowns of the women. The gilded brass of the ormolu furniture mounts caught the candlelight and threw it about the room in tiny glints. On the back wall, the green haircloth sofas were arranged side by side. Mary smiled and kept smiling, scanning the crowd. Most of the men were looking at Abigale admiringly.

Just then the front door opened again and Florence brought in another group of officers, resplendent in their scarlet coats and gorgets. Mary recognized the doctor among them and felt a rush of relief. He had come.

"He's here," Abigale whispered.

Mary glanced at her, following her shining eyes. Abigale was looking directly at the doctor, and he was returning her gaze, smiling.

"I'll be back in a moment, Mary," her father whispered and she nodded as he slipped his arm from beneath her hand. Abigale was still staring at the doctor.

Mary held her breath, willing her sister to notice any of the other half-dozen men in the room who were trying to catch her eye. This was going to make everything much harder.

A little gasp went up from the company and Mary turned to see her mother making a grand entrance to the greetings and compliments of everyone in the room. She wore all white, gilded at the edges of her petticoats and along the surplice bodice and hem. She glowed with milky pearls and a diamond comb set in her shining white wig. She caught Mary's eyes and smiled, giving her a meaningful look. Mary knew what it meant. Her mother wanted her to enjoy this evening, to have fun. But all she could think about was making sure that, somehow, William got help.

CHAPTER NINE

The harpist, the violinist, and the pianist arrived about an hour late. With the ease and calm that people often noticed and admired in her, Mary's mother sent them upstairs to the ballroom to ready their instruments and themselves. Since she had not allowed her concern over their lateness to show, and had not made a fuss upon their arrival, the party proceeded smoothly.

Laughter and good-natured jests erupted first in one corner of the room, then another. The dark wine was poured and the cut-glass pitchers of brandy and cider cast amber shards of light on the snow-white damask tablecloths.

The tables in the back parlor had been laid with care. Guests drifted back and forth from the food to the conversation in the front parlor. Mary had stayed close to her mother, speaking only when people questioned her about her sewing or her French lessons or made some other polite inquiry. Distracted, Mary let her mother lead her along, walking the gauntlet of the seated guests. Conversations overlapped and flowed, one into the next, swelling and fading as they went.

"White? For the whole bedchamber?" This was from a matronly woman Mary did not recognize. Several of the younger women laughed politely at her exaggerated expression. Mary's mother smiled. "Of course, Harriet. White. And only very thin bed curtains. It's all the fashion now. Mosquito netting and nothing more."

The woman named Harriet pressed a hand to her ample bosom and shook her head. "I could not sleep in a draft. Bed curtains are needed to prevent illness. It isn't a matter of *fashion*."

Mary's mother reached out to pat Harriet's shoulder. The older woman shook her head again, her piled hair a fraction of a second behind, swaying dangerously. Around her neck a string of garnets glowed like warm wine in the candlelight.

Mary looked back at Abigale for the twentieth time. She was still standing beside the doctor. Her colonel had arrived, too, and the two men flanked her like redcoated bookends. Abigale seemed content to be pressed between them, smiling at one, then the other, laughing with ladylike merriment at what each one said.

"Why don't you go and join your sister," Mary's mother said in her ear. Mary shook her head, but her mother nudged her insistently. "You don't belong with me, talking to old women about bed curtains all night long. Go, join the young people."

Mary shook her head again, but her mother had taken her arm and was marching her toward Abigale. Without hurrying, and acknowledging every guest she passed, Mary's mother guided her around the end chair nearest the fireplace, then across the room to the doorway where Abigale stood prettily, charming her officers.

As they got closer, Mary realized that the doctor and the colonel were only two out of five or six. The others were clumped loosely nearby, some of them talking to one another, casting sidelong glances at Abigale every few seconds. Mary wanted to get the doctor's attention, but this wasn't the way to do it. What could she say to him with Abigale and the others standing so close by? Mary balked.

"Mother, please. No one here wants to talk to me . . ."

"Nonsense. Just be polite. You may leave them any time you wish. But take a moment, please. Abigale will help you."

Abigale looked up at the sound of her name. She smiled at her mother and Mary, then a look of impatience flitted across her features. An instant later, the smile was back.

"I believe you have met my sister Mary," she said. "This is Dr. Morris, and Colonel Reddingcote . . ." Looking at Mary, she finished the introductions with three or four more of the men's names.

Mary mumbled and ducked her head.

"You look very pretty this evening, Mary," Dr. Morris said kindly. "I am sorry that our bringing the wounded men has interrupted your entertainment."

"A ball is hardly as important as someone being hurt," Mary answered without thinking. Then she blushed. She sounded like one of the flirting girls in the room. He would probably think she was trying to make him feel important. But he nodded gravely.

"I certainly think so. But most do not." He waved broadly at the room. "I have seen many men die in the past two days and this . . ." He trailed off.

"I suppose I have no right to criticize. I am here, after all."

"You were kind to come," Abigale said. Her colonel was fidgeting, trying to stand at an angle that would force her to look at him. She shifted slightly, almost turning her back. He made a sudden departure for the punch table, softening her rudeness. Mary heard her mother make a tiny sound, one that she was sure Abigale heard and understood. Abigale called after the colonel, asking him to bring her a glass of the punch.

Mary's mother gave a tiny nod. "We don't wish to be rude to any guest," she murmured, then turned, smiling, as someone called her name.

Mary watched, wishing everyone would just disappear except Dr. Morris. She looked up to find him regarding her with serious eyes. "Abigale says she will play pianoforte this evening. Will you be playing, too?"

Mary couldn't help but smile. He was trying so hard to be cordial, to pay attention to Abigale's plain younger sister. It was obvious that he was a very kind man. Perhaps she could trust him. She had to do *something*.

"Everyone? Excuse my intrusion, please."

Mary looked up to see her mother standing in the doorway, holding a small candle tree high in her right hand. "Dancing will begin upstairs."

A rustling of silk and lace began. Florence and Emily stood by to pull the chairs back close to the walls as they were vacated. For those who remained seated, a fresh round of jelly glasses had been brought from the kitchen. They had been set in front of the short, molded bayberry candles so that the light shone through the colored ribbons.

Mary felt a polite touch on her shoulder. The doctor was offering her his arm. She looked about wildly and saw the colonel with Abigale, who walked with her head held as high as a bloom on a swaying stem. Mary's palms felt damp. If she was going to trust Dr. Morris, now was the time to speak. There were a dozen or more lovely young women in the room, but kind Dr. Morris was singling her out simply because she stood nearby.

Mary felt flushed and clumsy as she took his arm. He walked very slowly, allowing her to collect her petticoats and her wits as they joined the upstairs procession. Talk and laughter swirled about them. Mary looked up at Dr. Morris, then back down at the stairs, afraid she would trip and fall. In a few seconds they would be at the top. Then, as couples formed for the first minuet, he would seek out a dancing partner and she might not be able to talk to him again before the evening was over. She struggled to find a way to begin. They were crossing the landing now, the gliding whisper of silk underlying the lively banter of the party.

"May I take advantage of your kindness?" Mary began. He bent closer. He had not heard her.

"Will you come into the yard with me later?"

She saw his surprise and shook her head. "No, no. Please don't think that. I only want you to do me a kindness. As a doctor."

Dr. Morris's eyebrows went up and Mary shook her head again, blushing hotly. "Not me. I am not ill. Someone . . . someone is hurt."

They were just topping the stairs and he led her to one side of the ballroom doors. There he leaned down to peer into her face.

"Who is hurt? And where?"

Mary looked past him, afraid to explain any further. People flowed past in a merry flood of rich colors and perfumes. There were gasps and appreciative exclamations from the guests as they came into the glimmer of the ballroom's polished floor and dancing candle chandeliers.

"A Continental soldier," Mary finally whispered. "My brother." She paused, staring into his eyes, trying to see if she had made an awful mistake in trusting him.

Dr. Morris stood tall again, glancing about. Mary held her breath. The war was the war, whether he liked it or not, and treating enemy soldiers was not his job.

"Please," Mary said quietly. She wasn't sure he had heard, but he bent close to her again. "Please don't tell my father. Or anyone."

"Is he dying?"

Mary looked away. "I pray not. I don't know. He spoke to me."

"Where is he?" Dr. Morris was gripping her arm firmly, drawing her to one side.

"In our stable. My father must not know," Mary repeated. "Nor anyone else."

Dr. Morris smiled at a jest made by someone going past. Mary didn't hear the remark and smiled anyway, hoping it hadn't been bawdy—a joke about the doctor attending such a young girl. He looked back down at her. "I will see him. Can we get out of the house without drawing attention?" He glanced down and Mary nodded.

"Yes. If we meet in the downstairs hall. There are no candles there. We can go by the kitchen without the servants knowing, if we are careful, then out the back door. I will show you the way."

He smiled at her. "In a quarter hour then. I will dance once, then slip away."

"You are very kind," Mary said, and her eyes flooded with tears.

Dr. Morris looked at her intently. "Little Mary, if half the women of the colonies and England were as tenderhearted as you are, there would be no war. Which would suit me fine."

"William is good and brave," Mary said, without knowing that she was going to say it. "And he is so hurt . . ." Her voice failed her and she could only stand, her face turned, fighting her tears.

Dr. Morris took her hands and squeezed them gently. "I only hope there is something I can do for him. A quarter hour, then?" Mary nodded and watched him as he bowed politely, taking his leave. He made his way into the ballroom just as the harpist began the first piece, a liquid cascade of notes.

Mary moved to stand just inside the doors. The dancers paired up quickly. The rich colors of the women's dresses, her mother's startling white silk, and the flickering orange gold of the candles made a nearly magical scene. And everywhere, spattered across the swirl and rustle of the many colored gowns, were the deep red coats of the British officers.

CHAPTER TEN

Mary watched the dancers. Abigale had been claimed by an officer Mary didn't recognize. He was tall and handsome, but he danced without grace and she could tell that Abigale was uncomfortable; she kept glancing around, aware of who might be watching. Her eyes met Mary's and she smiled as her partner led her past the doorway. But the smile faded quickly as the officer missed the music and Abigale had to hurry a step or two to catch up.

Mary saw her parents dancing on the far side of the room, gazing into each other's eyes as they stepped and spun. Her mother looked stately, the white gown standing out from the others, her hemline sparkling with its gold-threaded embroidery. Her father's white silk stockings looked striking with his dark breeches and waistcoat. His wig set off his appearance of formal elegance.

"You look very pretty, Mistress Mary."

Mary started and turned to see Benjamin, her father's clerk. He was carrying a tray of sweetmeats and cheese.

"I thank you for the compliment," she said politely. "I didn't know you were to serve tonight."

He looked glum. "Nor did I. But your mother asked the favor, and I could hardly turn her down." He dipped a little half bow and went on, circulating through the guests who were not yet dancing, offering the food this way and that.

Mary glanced behind herself. The landing was clear of people. Her parents were lost in dance and Abigale was preoccupied with her unreliable partner. There would be no shortage of volunteers to replace him at music's end. Mary looked around for the doctor and finally saw him just as the minuet ended. He bowed to Polly Grand, a blond friend of Abigale's. Then he turned and looked toward the door. Without meaning to, Mary met his eyes. He gave her a tiny nod, then escorted Polly to the far end of the ballroom, as though he were searching for a new partner among the crowd standing there.

Mary surveyed the room quickly, to make sure that neither of her parents was looking for her, then she stepped back out of the doorway and slowly walked toward the head of the stairs. Emily was snuffing the candles on the landing candle tree, deftly trimming the smoking wicks. Mary nodded politely at the people who passed her, on their way upstairs from the food and wine in the back parlor, or from conversation in the front parlor.

As Mary passed, Florence was snuffing candles in the front parlor, intent on her task. There were so many candles lit, the two women would be running to keep up with the wick trimming as the evening went on.

Emily came down the stairs just behind Mary and began rearranging food on the back parlor tables. Mary paused until Florence and Emily were absorbed in their work, then she slipped past. Neither one looked up.

Once Mary was away from the bright candles of the party, the hallway was dark—as dark as ink. Sometimes the shadows in the unlit parts of the house frightened her, but tonight Mary welcomed them. She stopped just short of the kitchen door. Rachel was humming to herself as she almost always did.

The grotesque shadows thrown on the wall by the hearth fire made Rachel seem a monstrous form, a distorted, flickering silhouette. Mary leaned against the wall, her eyes moving from the far end of the hallway to the kitchen doorway, then back.

Florence was coming, carrying a candleholder. The amber globe of light from the flame showed her face, tense and tired. She walked as briskly as she could without putting out the flame, carrying the candle in one hand and a heavy silver tray in the other. Mary hesitated an instant, then went quickly and silently farther down the hall, tiptoeing past the kitchen door. Rachel's humming continued undisturbed. Mary turned to see Florence still walking toward her, her expression unchanged.

"You should see them," Florence said as she went into the kitchen, passing within a few feet of where Mary stood holding her breath.

Rachel's melody stopped. "See who?"

Mary could see, at an angle, about half the kitchen. Florence had set down her candleholder beside the tray on the sideboard. She pulled her skirts out from her hips and began a heavy-footed minuet, mincing and smiling, making wicked fun of the exaggerated manners of the ladies. "And our Abigale is among the worst. Flirting and simpering like that. I am surprised her mother allows it."

"Her mother encourages it," Rachel said mildly. "And so would you. It's her best chance to find a husband who will be an important man in the colonies."

Florence let her skirts fall straight. "What colonies? If you ask me, old George Three is about to lose his footing here." Rachel did not answer. Florence clicked her tongue and shook her head. "You know what I mean and you agree with me, too. You're just afraid to say it aloud."

Another long pause made Mary wonder if Rachel was ever going to answer. When she did, her voice was taut, strained. "When I bought my freedom and came to Philadelphia with my Harold, I left my whole family behind. I suppose this war would mean more to me if I thought any of them would win anything by it. But they will still be slaves whichever way it falls out."

Florence made a small sound of apology, then Mary heard the tray bumping against the sideboard. Florence was drying it with a soft cloth before she took another load of food to the tables. The shadows shifted as Florence picked up her candle and went into the storeroom with the tray.

The sound of cautious footsteps made Mary look back down the hall. It was a man, alone. Dr. Morris? She watched the advancing figure, like a black paper cutout against the bright rectangle of the far end of the hall. He was wearing a military jacket, but she couldn't tell more than that from his outline. Whoever it was, Mary knew it was impossible for him to see her, so she waited.

The man advanced slowly, as though uncertain about where he was going. As he got closer, he hesitated, as if he were having second thoughts about going anywhere at all. Rachel was singing again more loudly, her voice low and liquid. He came closer, then stopped again when he was ten or twelve feet away from where Mary stood in the darkness. He was obviously reluctant to pass the kitchen door.

Mary made a tiny hissing sound, just loud enough for the man to hear, if he was alert. He turned his head sharply, then stopped and waited silently.

Florence came clumping out of the storeroom, back into the kitchen, the tray full of jelly glasses. She set it down on the sideboard and went back for her candleholder. "I'll just leave this here."

Mary saw Rachel look up. "The fire's enough. Blow it out." The light in the kitchen dimmed and Mary smelled the unpleasant odor of tallow smoke.

"I wonder how late they'll keep at it," Florence said. When Rachel did not answer, Florence muttered to herself. "Well, it will be a while still, that much is certain."

Mary looked up the hall. The man was close, a few paces away. "Mary?" he whispered.

"Yes."

The faint light from the kitchen fire outlined the doctor's profile as he came forward, passing the kitchen doorway in one quick stride.

"This way," Mary whispered.

In the kitchen, Florence sighed loudly, then yawned and stretched, her back to the doorway. "I'd best get back with these glasses. And it's time to snuff the downstairs candles again."

Mary took Dr. Morris's arm and pulled him a little farther down the hall. Together they stood still in the darkness as Florence came out of the kitchen, walking slowly and carefully, carrying the tray of jelly glasses. Mary waited, her hand on the doctor's arm, until Florence emerged into the light at the far end of the hall. From the kitchen, Rachel's voice rose as she began to sing a hymn.

"Take me to your brother now," Dr. Morris whispered.

"I only pray William still lives," Mary said softly, admitting her fear. Dr. Morris touched her arm. She led him to the back door, then stood aside as he lifted the bar and pushed it open. Once out on the porch, Mary closed the door behind them, hoping no one would notice that the bar was drawn while they were in the carriage house.

Mary led Dr. Morris down the back steps. The air was chill, the stars above sparkled like a scatter of cut glass.

"I brought a candle," the doctor whispered. "I stole it from the parlor. But is there anywhere to light it?"

Mary felt foolish. She should have thought to bring light. "Samuel builds a little fire in the carriage room hearth. But the loft will be dark as coal." Mary could hear faint strains of harp and violin from the ballroom on the second floor, then a muted burst of laughter. She glanced up at the windows. The fitting room and all the bedchambers were dark, their windows opaque. No candles flickered at this end of the house at all.

"The moon will give us a little light," Dr. Morris said quietly.

"I know the way," Mary told him. He offered her his arm again and they started across the gardens. Mary had to pick her way past the bare-branched pear trees, trying not to snag her gown. Her heart beat heavily with fear. What if William was worse? What if there was nothing Dr. Morris could do?

At the carriage house wall, Mary stopped, bending awkwardly against her stays to find a tiny pebble. She threw it in a high arc so that it landed on the roof. She could hear it rattling down over the roof tiles.

"Who are you signaling?" Dr. Morris whispered.

"David, our stable boy. He got William to move from the garden shed to his loft."

"Must we wait for him?" Dr. Morris asked. Mary stooped and found another pebble. She threw it higher this time. It clattered downward, unreasonably loud in the quiet, cold air. Mary held her breath. Long silent seconds ticked past.

"Mistress Mary!"

Mary nearly cried out in relief at the sound of Davey's hushed greeting. "We must be quiet," she whispered. "I don't want to wake the coachman."

"This way, Mistress Mary." Mary moved toward Davey's voice. He was standing in the wide carriage house doorway. As they got a little closer, she heard his quick, startled breath as he saw Dr. Morris. Even in the blue and gray shadows of the night there was no mistaking the uniform of a British officer.

"He's a doctor, Davey," Mary whispered quickly. "He says he will help William."

Dr. Morris nodded. "If he can be helped."

"This way, sir," Davey said, turning without another word. He led them into the carriage house, moving silently. Mary gathered her petticoats in one hand, lifting them higher than was proper. The stable straw and dust would cling, telling the tale of her absence.

"Here's the ladder," Davey breathed. Mary could just make it out. The moonlight was nearly shut out of the carriage house.

"Is there a fireplace somewhere close? Can we light a candle?" Dr. Morris asked in a barely audible voice.

"I thought to bring a little tin of coals up there," Davey said, "when I came to bed. And I have a little tallow candle stub."

Mary felt her stomach tighten in spite of her relief that Davey had thought of light. "Coals? In the hayloft?" Fires terrified her. They had had two small ones in the past year, one in the kitchen and one in the sitting room when a spark had leapt from the chimney and landed in a woolen rug.

"We will be very careful," the doctor said in a low voice. "Can you manage the ladder?"

Mary nodded and began to climb. Her bulky petticoats made it difficult, but she reached the top and stumbled only a little as she stepped into the hay.

"Davey?" It was William's voice and Mary's heart leapt with joy and relief.

"William?" she said softly.

"Here, Mary."

Without waiting for Davey or Dr. Morris, Mary went toward her brother. He spoke again when she got close, saying her name in a thin, low voice that frightened her. Mary knelt in the hay beside him, forgetful of her gown, her shoes, of everything but her fear for him.

"The coals are here, sir," Mary heard Davey whisper.

A few seconds later, a tiny flame sprang up from a straw pressed against the coals. Davey lifted it carefully to light the candle in Dr. Morris's hand.

"Who is . . . ?" William said, raising his head, then coughed. "Mary . . . what have you done?"

"Saved your life, perhaps," Dr. Morris said quietly, crossing the loft. "I am a doctor. I am here to see to your wounds." He handed the candle to Mary and sank to his knees beside William. "Hold that light steady, Mary. Turn your head if you cannot look, but do not drop it or we will have a fire yet."

Mary nodded, swallowing. In the candlelight all she could see was the impossibly bright red of Dr. Morris's officer's jacket and the duller crimson of William's bloody bandages.

CHAPTER ELEVEN

"His wounds are bad enough," Dr. Morris said, rewrapping the last strand of bandage. He stood to take the candle from Mary. "But I have seen men with worse recover if they were cared for, kept warm, and fed broth and tea."

"You will not tell my father," William interrupted in a rasping whisper. "I didn't mean to come here. I was stupid with pain."

"William—" Mary began, but he cut her off, his voice weak and barely audible.

"He said I was no longer his son. So be it."

Dr. Morris leaned to whisper in Mary's ear.

"He either gets care or he will die. He might die anyway. Surely your father would take him in? Or is he as stubborn as his son?"

Mary recalled her father's hard, determined face when he'd talked about William's joining Washington's army. She shrugged, unsure. Her father loved William, even if he hated the rebels' cause. Still, if she tried to tell him now, tonight . . . ? "My father could hardly welcome William home with half of General Howe's officers here."

"He must be moved inside, somehow. And soon." Dr. Morris rubbed his hand over his face, then shrugged sadly. "Pity he is not in the right army. He could share the attic room with the other two."

Davey had come to stand beside them. He looked down at William. "He's been asleep more than awake. It wears him down to talk."

Mary took a breath, then let it out, an idea growing in her mind. "You could say he's another British soldier and we could cover his face somehow . . . and just take him upstairs. They are all dancing. They won't notice too much."

"What are you . . . whispering about?" William rasped, then fell silent again.

"I think," the doctor breathed, too low for William to hear, "that it might work. But he won't stand for it if he wakens." He gestured at William, who had closed his eyes again.

Mary shook her head, trying to think. How could they get William back down the ladder? She looked up at Dr. Morris, holding the candle to one side so that she could lean close enough to speak into his ear. "Do you have a medicine that would make him sleep?"

Dr. Morris nodded. "Laudanum. I could not give him much, just enough to get him inside. But, Mary, your father . . ."

Mary nodded. "He might never forgive me. But what choice is there? I cannot believe that Father would put William out once he is inside. He will see how hurt William is."

Dr. Morris turned to Davey. "My medicines are in a leather purse in the second carriage waiting in the drive. The coachman's name is Henry. Tell him I sent you for the bag and the stretcher. Tell Henry he is to help you bring it. Henry has a brother in Washington's army," he added when Davey hesitated. "Tell him what we are about. He'll help."

Davey nodded and disappeared into the darkness beyond the little pool of light around the candle. Mary heard him go down the ladder, then his quick footfalls as he started across the yard.

"It hurts," William said. He groaned and

turned, but he did not really awaken.

"Will this cause . . ." Mary began, but she didn't know how to finish. Dr. Morris was looking at her quizzically, so she took a deep breath and began again. "Will helping us cause you trouble?"

He shrugged. "If your father reported it to my superiors perhaps. But once we get William upstairs, once the ball is over and the officers gone, it is my bet that your father will be glad his son still lives."

If he does live, Mary thought, but she would not say it aloud. Sounds from below made her turn. Dr. Morris handed her the candle, then went to the ladder and started down. Mary could hear his voice murmuring, then a harsh whisper in answer. A moment later, Dr. Morris was back beside her, a dark leather case in his hands. Mary lifted the candle higher so he could see. He unbuckled the bag quickly and withdrew a small, stoppered bottle. Without a word of warning, he knelt and lifted William's head. William's eyes fluttered open. He tried to speak but Dr. Morris tipped the bottle against his lips. Startled, William swallowed, then coughed. The doctor patted his arm. "That ought to help you a bit. Now, just lie back."

William lay back down, looking at Dr. Morris for a half a minute before he closed his eyes again.

Mary wanted to ask how long it would take the laudanum to work, but she didn't dare. From the foot of the ladder, she heard a shuffling sound, then silence.

The candle flickered. Mary licked her thumb and forefinger, then pinched the wick end quickly to rid it of the little tail of ashen snuff that could make it gutter and go out. Mary stared into the candle to avoid watching William's pain-contorted face. The little orange and blue flame danced, even in the still air of the loft. Twice Mary looked up at Dr. Morris, and he nodded reassurance. The third time he leaned close to her to whisper. "Look. See how he's resting now? The pain is bothering him less."

Mary looked at William's face. It was true. His features had relaxed; his lips had parted and his breathing was more even. Dr. Morris bent to touch William's arm, then his cheek. There was no response. "I think we can move him now."

Mary snuffed the candle again and it flickered. She held her breath, afraid it would go out, but it did not. Dr. Morris went to the head of the ladder and whispered. "Henry? I will lower him down to you. Come halfway up at least, and be ready." Then he came back to stand beside Mary. "Light my way as much as you can. We will go slowly. With luck we will not wake William or the other coachman." He looked at Mary. "Steady with the candle, Mary. You are a brave girl."

Mary did not feel brave. She felt terrified that something would go wrong. But she only nodded and raised the candle, stepping back. Dr. Morris squatted and slid his hands beneath William, as though he were a sleeping child. Grunting with effort, the doctor stood up slowly, then swayed a moment on his feet before he took his first careful step toward the ladder. William did not rouse. His arms hung loosely.

Mary walked slowly forward, trying to tilt the candle a little to let Dr. Morris see the mounds of hay he had to walk across. The hot tallow dripped onto her hand, but she did not waver, biting the inside of her cheek against the sudden pain and holding the candle a little higher so Dr. Morris could see the trapdoor as he shifted William's weight. Deftly, at the head of the ladder, the doctor let William's limp body slide, feet first, to a standing position. Then, before William could collapse to the hay, Dr. Morris moved his hands to William's sides and embraced him, lifting him carefully and easing forward until William's feet dangled over the ladder. Then he lowered him, and Mary held her breath.

"I have him, but don't let him go yet." It was Henry's grating whisper.

"There. Easy." Dr. Morris lowered William a little farther, bending almost double. Then he knelt, his hands beneath William's arms. After a moment, he straightened and Mary heard whispers from below. Dr. Morris turned. "They have him on the stretcher. Let me take the candle."

Mary handed it to him, suddenly aware that her hand hurt from gripping it so tightly for so long. She flexed her fingers, trying to ease the tension in her muscles, then started down the ladder, fighting her petticoats. About halfway she felt a hand on her waist, steadying her. As she stepped from the ladder to the ground she whispered her thanks to Henry. Then she saw William, lying on the stretcher. Davey was bent over him, doing something she couldn't make out in the darkness. Dr. Morris came down the ladder. He had put out the candle.

"Let's carry him in, then," Dr. Morris whispered as he alighted. "And once we get inside, not a word from any of you. I will do the explaining. And if I must lie, don't any of you gainsay me, not with a word or by a frown. Agreed?" He waited for them all to nod, then he looked at Davey. "I am sure tomorrow's work won't be lighter for all the sleep you have lost."

"William has been very good to me, sir. I would lose a great deal more than sleep to help him." Davey's whisper was edged with emotion.

Mary felt her eyes sting at Davey's brave words. She reached out and took his hand for an instant. Then she looked down at the pale outline of William's face again.

Dr. Morris positioned himself at the end of the stretcher. "Henry. Through the side yard to the front. We will need our carriage robe to cover his face. Go now, Mary," Dr. Morris added gently. "Back the way we came, and try to look as though you are enjoying the party."

His barely audible words hung in the air for a second. Mary looked once more at William, then fled back across the gardens.

CHAPTER TWELVE

Mary went up the steps, then stood for a few seconds, brushing at her skirt, before she went inside. Her hands were trembling and she felt almost sick as she lowered the lock bar and leaned against the closed door.

Over the sound of her own heart Mary could hear Rachel, still singing in the kitchen. The hallway was empty. The rectangle of candlelight at the far end looked foreign, unfamiliar. She could hear the music upstairs and a sudden burst of laughter from the back parlor.

Mary took a wary step forward, then another,

her eye on the kitchen door. Rachel was facing the hearth, turning the spit to roast a pork loin evenly as Mary glided past. Mary could smell the thyme she had seasoned it with. This was another of Mary's mother's touches. Freshly roasted meat was brought out at intervals during the entertainment.

Mary walked fast once she was past the kitchen. She emerged from the dark hallway into the light, looking quickly into the back parlor, then through the wide, open doors of the front parlor. There were people in both rooms, but no one seemed to notice her as she turned the corner and went up the stairway.

Halfway up, Mary noticed a few strands of hay clinging to her hem. She walked close enough to the balustrade to brush them off against the polished wood. Any second now there would be a sharp knock on the front door. Mary turned toward the ballroom, stopping in the doorway to watch.

The music was spritely, the harpist's hands a blur of motion over the strings. Two long lines of dancers stepped to the music, the women's gowns sparkling in the light of the chandelier candles. Mary saw her father and Abigale, opposite each other. Mary's father was beaming, obviously proud of his beautiful daughter.

"Mary!"

Mary saw her mother smiling, walking toward her. "Where have you been? Downstairs?"

Mary nodded, hoping her mother wouldn't ask anything else.

"I have been looking for you. Abigale played beautifully. Have you danced?"

Mary started to shake her head, but the abrupt knocking at the front door made her mother turn and look toward the stairs. "Who do you suppose? Late arrivals?"

Mary didn't answer. Her heart was pounding again, and without meaning to, she started walking. Her mother swirled her gown, turning, and followed. "Mary? Have you seen Abigale dancing? She looks like a vision this evening. I'm not sure where the doctor she was so taken with went. He must be with the men talking in the back parlor. But there have been three or four others who are certainly dashing and . . ."

Mary's mother's voice stopped as they reached the landing and looked downstairs. Florence, a little behind her, then the stretcher came into view. Mary stood to one side, unable to take her eyes off the prone form of her brother, covered entirely by a carriage robe. He was completely still.

"I am so very sorry, madam," Dr. Morris said, looking up the stairs at Mary's mother. "I had little warning of this myself. But I beg your favor, if I could place this soldier with the others?"

Mary's mother nodded vaguely, then with a little more certainty. "Of course. Of course. But please, Doctor, if you could come quickly so that the dancers are not too much disturbed?"

Dr. Morris bowed and said something to Henry. They raised the stretcher and started up the stairs.

"What's this?"

Mary whirled at the sound of her father's voice. The music had stopped and people were coming out of the ballroom to watch. Mary's father came to stand beside her.

"Kind sir," Dr. Morris said as Henry stepped onto the landing, "I have asked madam if we might place this poor soldier with the other two."

Mary's father nodded.

"I asked him to hurry past," Mary's mother said quickly. The crowd was gathering, drawn out of the ballroom by the commotion on the landing.

Mary's father turned and she saw him take in the growing throng of guests. He leaned forward and squeezed Mary's shoulder. "Light their way up, will you, Mary? I will get the music started again." He stepped back, taking a candle from the wall sconce to hand to Mary. "Florence? Attend the candles in the ballroom, please. I don't want any going out." He leaned close to

Mary's mother to say something, then he was gone.

Mary's mother gestured, asking the guests to move back so that the stretcher could be brought through. Mary heard the music start again, a lively rhythm, played loudly.

"Thank you for leading us up," Dr. Morris said, sharply enough to make Mary stop staring at the stretcher. She began to walk, her knees stiff with fear, her throat dry. She tried to look into the ballroom as they passed it, but could not see her father. Within a few seconds, they were beyond the crowd, heading up the hallway that led past her own room. William stirred on the cot and the carriage robe slipped a little, showing his forehead.

"I think he will wake up before too long," Dr. Morris said, then raised his voice a little. "Go up this last stairway slowly, Henry. It's steeper and narrower." Henry did not comment as Mary hurried around them to open the door. She watched as the two men maneuvered the stretcher, with Dr. Morris raising his end to chest height, trying to keep it level as they started upward. Where the carriage robe had slipped aside, William's skin looked too white, cold. Mary wished they could take him into the kitchen, where the heat from the hearth would warm him. She got a sudden idea and glanced down the hall. No one else was coming.

Dr. Morris and Henry had topped the short,

steep flight of stairs when Mary started up after them. They set down the stretcher and Dr. Morris was about to open the door to Mary and Abigale's old room, but she stopped him.

"There's another chamber, smaller, but it's kept clean for mother's linens. The hearth chimney passes through it and there's an old bed. It was the sickroom for all of us. It's much warmer."

"Where?" Dr. Morris looked at her over his shoulder. She pointed to the very end of the hall. The two men carried the stretcher to the doorway, then set it down. Dr. Morris opened the door, reaching to take the candle from Mary. He peered in. "This will be perfect." He lit a candle in a holder on the little table to the left of the door. Then he handed Mary's candle back to her. "Run and get him some broth while we move him to the bed."

Mary nodded but watched while Dr. Morris uncovered William—his skin was even paler than it had looked by moonlight. William groaned and moved restlessly. Mary felt a chill pass through her heart. She left, walking as fast as she could without putting out her candle. At the foot of the stairs, she fit it into a wall sconce. There was no reason to carry it all the way downstairs.

Passing the ballroom, Mary hurried, hoping that neither of her parents would see her. No one called out and she started downstairs.

The kitchen seemed impossibly warm and bright as Mary came in from the dark hallway. Rachel turned and smiled at her.

"What sends you here, Mistress Mary? The dance cannot be over yet?"

Mary shook her head. "Is there broth? I need some meat broth for . . . one of the wounded soldiers." Mary prayed Rachel would not notice the awkward pause in her sentence, or her nervousness.

Rachel nodded. "Of course. I made it for a gravy earlier and had a bit too much. Can you carry a tray? Or I could find Emily?"

Mary shook her head. "I can carry it. Perhaps a bit of bread, too, Rachel."

"Yes, mistress," Rachel said pleasantly. She set about pouring a bowl of broth and warming the bread. It seemed to take forever. Mary paced back and forth across the kitchen, too nervous to sit down or to talk. Finally Rachel handed her the tray.

On her way back upstairs, Mary hurried past the front parlor doors, then slowed down, trying hard not to spill any of the broth. She walked as quickly as she could past the ballroom, not daring to look in the doors. The violins were tremulous, hovering above the harp's melody. Mary wondered if William was waking up. The instant he heard the music and opened his eyes he would know where he was. And he was going to be angry. If their father put him out, he would never forgive her. Somehow she had to convince her father to let William stay. At the foot of the third-story stairs, Mary got her candle from the sconce and put it on the tray.

When she got back up to the tiny room, Henry had gone. The candle flickered on a tin stand on the table. Dr. Morris was sitting in the only chair. William had turned and was facing the wall, his legs drawn up.

"I have the broth," Mary said quietly.

William stirred. "Mary? Is that you?"

Mary came to stand beside the bed. "Here," Dr. Morris said from behind her. He was pulling the chair back, setting the table closer. She placed the tray on it, then sank to her knees beside the bed.

William turned over, wincing. His eyes were deep, a little unfocused. "Mary?"

"I brought you some broth, William. Dr. Morris says you must drink it." She twisted around to get the bowl from the tray.

"You will have to spoon it out for him," Dr. Morris said.

Mary nodded and touched the edge of the bowl to her own lips, tipping it to take a sip of the broth. It was not too hot. She filled the spoon, then held it out for William. He took it like an obedient child, looking at her closely. "Mary."

Dr. Morris smiled at Mary. "He is not quite

himself yet. But he soon will be. I looked at him again while you were gone. As I thought, the ball passed through his shoulder. His other wounds are from a bayonet and they are serious but not necessarily mortal. He has a good nurse. With God's help he will live." He stood up. "I am going to look in on the other two." He took the candle from the tray.

Mary smiled at him, then looked down again. She spooned up more broth for her brother. He was watching her intently, his eyes still soft and unsure. "It is good broth, Mary." He sounded like a boy of ten, not a young man of eighteen. "I am home?" William asked. "Or is this a dream?"

"It's not a dream," Mary told him. "You were out in the stable, then we brought you inside."

William's brow clouded. "But Father said—"

"He doesn't know you are here."

William sighed heavily and closed his eyes. "I am so tired. It hurts so much."

"You need to swallow more of the broth," Mary reminded him. She lifted the spoon. He opened his eyes and took another mouthful.

"I must go," William said. He tried to prop himself up on one elbow, then fell back. "Father did not want me here."

"Mary," Dr. Morris whispered urgently from the doorway. She looked up. "Your father is calling up the stairs."

Mary clambered to her feet, setting the bowl on the table. "Please, keep William here," she pleaded. Dr. Morris nodded. She went into the hall and ran for the stairs.

Her father was leaning into the doorway. He smiled up at her as she came down the steep steps. "Is the good doctor still up there?" He peered through the door and Mary was terrified that he was going to go up. Her heartbeat was so loud in her own ears that it seemed her father would have to notice it.

"I was just helping him a little. I brought broth for one of the soldiers. I would like to go back and—"

"It's time you joined the guests, Mary," her father said, taking her arm. He turned her firmly around and started her walking toward the ballroom. She could hear the music beginning. The violins soared, shimmering above the harpist's melody.

Mary tried to free her arm. "The man is quite hurt."

Her father held her tightly. "It is a shame these rebel fools will not end this war and admit their wrongdoing." He shook his head. "The leaders would hang, but the king would pardon the rest, I feel sure."

Mary couldn't respond. As they neared the ballroom, her father released her arm but took her hand. "Your mother is concerned about you," he said. "She thinks you are taking all this too much to heart."

Mary was barely listening to her father. All she could think about was William. When the drug had run its course, he might try to leave, and the effort might hurt him. How long would Dr. Morris stay upstairs? Mary looked up at her father. "Helping the hurt soldiers seems more important than dancing."

Her father pushed a curl back from her forehead. "Mary, dear. The doctor can do what is needed. I want you to stay with our guests." He began to pull her toward the ballroom. The glittering bouquet of gowns and red jackets dizzied her.

Mary shook her head. "Father," she said breathlessly. "I need to go back up."

He squeezed her hand. "No, Mary. Now let that be an end on this. Your mother wants you—"

"I do not want to dance, now," Mary said, too loudly. She saw a few people glance her way and she lowered her voice. "I would very much like to help the doctor," she pleaded.

"These soldiers are not proper companions for a girl your age," her father said. "They are likely ruffians, and hardly worth your concern."

"William is a soldier," Mary shot back at him. "Would you want someone to talk about him that way?" Mary saw her father stiffen.

"I have told you that I do not wish to hear that name," he whispered angrily. "Your mother has worked very hard to make this evening remarkable. Don't you think you are being selfish, Mary?" She stared at him as they stopped on the landing at the top of the stairs. How could she tell him? She had to, or William wouldn't get the kind of care that Dr. Morris had said might save his life.

"Answer me, Mary," her father said sternly.

"I think," Mary said as steadily as she could, "that someone being hurt is more important than all this." She gestured at the guests, the decorations. "What if it was William up there? Wouldn't you want someone to take care of him?" Before her father could scold her for using William's name again, Mary reached out and touched her fingers to his lips to silence him. "Think before you answer, Father."

Then, before he could react, Mary whirled around and ran back past the ballroom. She did not stop until she was at the foot of the narrow stairs.

Out of breath and sure that her father would follow her, Mary went up the steep steps. She could hear Dr. Morris's voice, then William's as she got closer. She heard boot heels coming up the stairs and turned to face her father as he came into the narrow hallway, red-faced and angry.

"When Father finds out I am here, he will throw me out," William was saying. His voice carried clearly into the hall. Mary saw the shock of recognition on her father's face.

"Listen, Father," Mary said. "If you love me at all, you will listen."

Her father narrowed his eyes.

"My arm is on fire," William said loudly. There was a scuffling sound. "I have to get up. I have to go before he finds me here."

"Your father will be happy that you are alive," Dr. Morris said. "Mary says he loves you dearly."

"He said I was no longer his son. That he did not want me home again, ever." William coughed. "I truly did not mean to come." His voice sank to a confused rasp. "Why did I come here?"

Dr. Morris's voice got a little louder. "William, men with wounds like yours can die if they aren't warm and cared for. You must rest."

"I would rather die than see Father's face. I cannot stand him hating me." William drew in a great, shuddering breath. "I would rather die than hear him say it again." He erupted into coughing.

Mary was watching her father. She saw the pain in his eyes, but his mouth was still a tense, thin line. "Does the war have to be fought here, too?" she whispered. "In our house?"

"This is the man they brought up? Our William?" He hissed the words.

Mary nodded. "He was in the stables. It was

too cold out there. Dr. Morris gave him laudanum or he would not have let us move him."

Mary's father looked incredulous. "This was Dr. Morris's idea?"

"No," Mary said quickly. "It was mine."

Slowly, her father shook his head.

"Where is Mary?" William was asking. Dr. Morris murmured some answer.

Mary's father patted her hand and started forward. Then he hesitated. Mary's heart hammered against her ribs. "If you make him leave, I will go with him," she said quietly.

Mary's father embraced her a moment, then held her back to look into her eyes. "Run, Mary, and tell your mother William is home. Don't frighten her with too much about his wounds." He blinked and Mary thought he was going to say more, but he did not.

Mary watched him go through the doorway. She stood still, her fists clenched, waiting for their angry words. When there was only silence, she peeked in.

Her father had taken her place beside the bed and he and William were looking at each other, neither one smiling, their faces grave. Dr. Morris was standing at the foot of the bed, his expression wary. As Mary watched, her father reached for the bowl of broth and lifted the spoon.

William seems better. He ate nearly a half bowl of broth last night and almost as much this morning. Dr. Morris says that is a very good sign. Rachel is making a grand fuss over him; the entire household is. Father says they will not argue about the war until William is well enough to stand it, which makes William smile.

Dr. Morris came to call this morning. He changed William's bandages, and those of the other two soldiers. They are both British, sent here to fight. John Heacock is the one who can walk. He spent half the morning in William's room. They talked about the battle and let me listen. It sounds, as they speak, that soldiers know very little about what is happening while they fight. John did say that the Chews' summer home was used as a fort by the British. Clivedon is a beautiful place and I hate the thought of cannon balls crashing through the roof.

This noon I saw Father talking to Davey. It worried me until I could ask Davey later. Father thanked him, he said, for his part in helping

William. I am so glad his bravery will not cost him.

Abigale is very happy to have William home and teases him that at her next ball, he must dance, not lie about all evening. Peale House feels cheerful this day. Mother walks about smiling at nothing. Even Florence is humming at her work. So we will have one peaceful, contented day. I cannot know how long the happiness will last with the war all around us, but I am very grateful. And now it is time to take William more broth. I will write again tomorrow.

Sometimes one day can change a life forever

Different girls,
living in different periods of America's past
reveal their hearts' secrets in the pages
of their diaries. Each one faces a challenge
that will change her life forever.
Don't miss any of their stories: